the

WAYPOINT

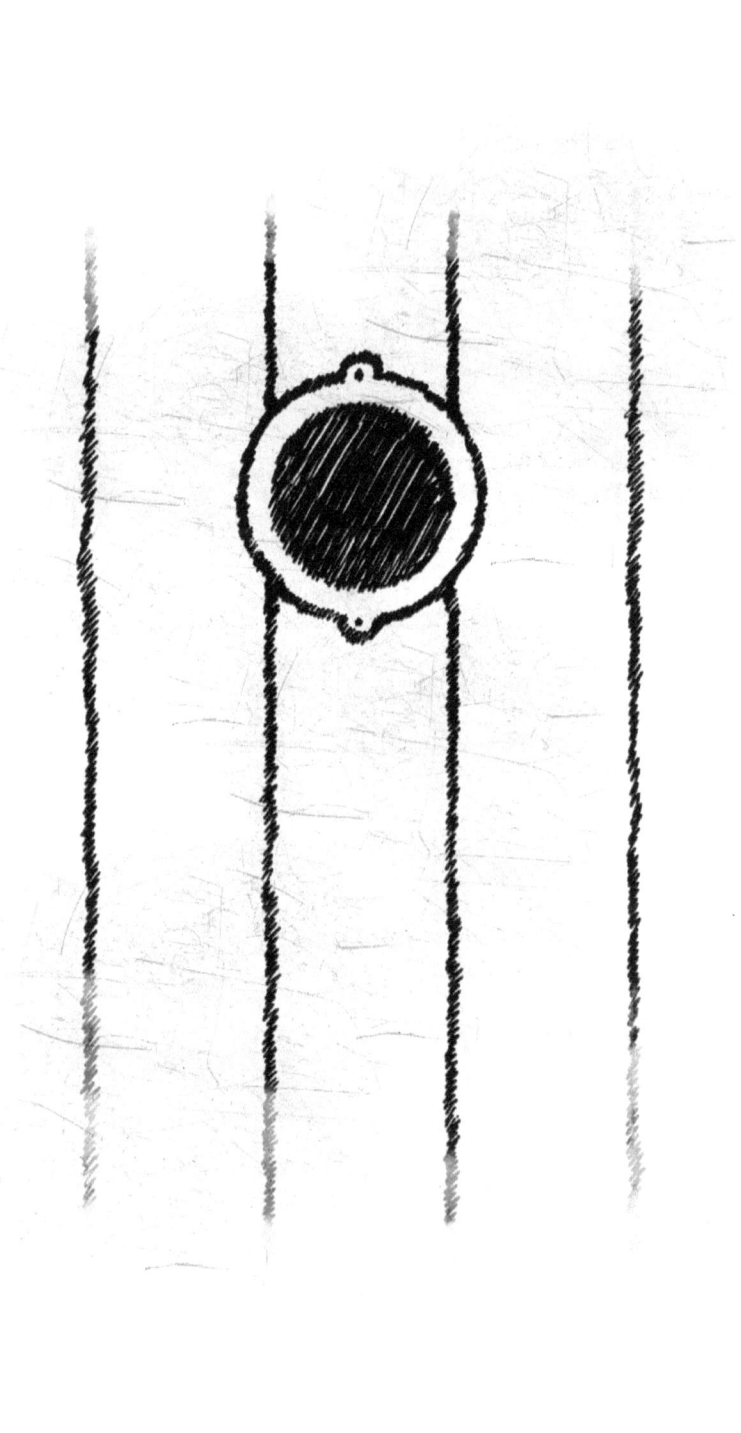

the
WAYPOINT

a novel

BEN HASKETT

Cover design by Ben Haskett. Many of the scribblings inside were drawn freehand, but the images for chapters one, fifteen, and sixteen, as well as pieces of the back cover, used existing works as a template.

First Printing: 2016

ISBN-13: 978-0692794975

ISBN-10: 0692794972

www.undinestudios.com

Thank you.

Stephanie Haskett, my wife
Nina Haskett, my mom
Aaron Haskett, my brother
Elizabeth Haskett, my sister
Katie Haskett, my sister
David Wheeler, David McMillan,
Jenna Swartzendruber, and
Dustin Oakley, my friends

You read my book and helped me make it better.

CHAPTER ONE: ACQUISITIONS

Gil Sanders raised his auction paddle and arched his eyebrows. The auctioneer quickly spotted him, indicating as much with an enthusiastic pair of finger guns, and exclaimed, "I've got $60 for the broiler! $60! Can I get $75 for the broiler?"

The auctioneer continued in this manner at a pace one would normally ascribe to auctioneers, darting his pointed hands over the group of attendees in the warehouse.

Gil turned to face his friend, Daryl—an overweight man in his mid-thirties, who wore a baseball cap seemingly glued to the top of his head. Grey stubble was slowly conquering his otherwise-black beard, which clung to a face aged by stress.

"Daryl, you should really think about bidding on something," Gil said.

Daryl grimaced. "Bid on what?" he asked, spreading out his arms. "What's here for me?"

"Bid on w—?" Gil stammered and shook his head, "It's a *restaurant* auction, Daryl. Literally anything. Think about bidding on the next thing they cart out here."

Daryl shook his head and chuckled nervously, "Yeah, no thanks, pal. Look, I'm down to hang out, but these places give me the creeps."

Gil raised his paddle again. It caught the attention of the auctioneer, who acknowledged him with another pair of finger guns before continuing his chant. Gil then continued as if there hadn't been a break in the conversation. "Come on, don't be dramatic. What's so awful about this? The restaurant goes out of business, and then they sell their stuff. I can't even tell you how much awesome stuff I've walked away with from these things."

"Going once!"

"Yeah, I know, Gil," Daryl admitted, rubbing the back of his neck. "I've been to your house, man. Many times. It's like a graveyard for failed businesses in there."

"Going twice!"

"You're so dramatic tonight! Look, I'm just saying I know things are getting rough. I heard about the gas range, and—"

"Sold! The broiler goes to Number 126 for $225!"

Gil looked at his auction paddle, which read 207. "Dammit, Daryl! I lost that one."

Daryl shoved his hands into his faded cargo shorts. He stared at Gil and responded sardonically, "Sorry, not sorry, Gil. What is that—one out of a dozen so far? I'm already not sure if you're gonna have enough room to sit in the driver's seat."

Gil scoffed, shook his head, and looked to the front of the warehouse. "I guess I can let that one go," he allowed.

Several attendants rolled out a lightly-used industrial gas range on dollies and parked it next to the auctioneer, who looked up and launched straight back into the bidding process.

With a coy smile, Gil exclaimed, "Finally! Daryl, I know you need this—you know it too! Come on, man, make a bid."

Daryl grimaced again. "Ugh, you knew this was going to be a part of the auction, didn't you? Did you really drag me all the way down here for this? No, I can fix the one I got. I don't want that range anyway—I *recognize* it, Gil." Daryl pointed to a forlorn man in the far corner of the warehouse. "Hell, I recognize its soon-to-be previous owner over there. His little bakery was in the same strip mall as my restaurant. You should know that, Gil—you kicked him out."

Gil considered this. True, as a commercial landlord, he'd had the ugly job of kicking the bakery owner out, but this had been a long time coming. The guy just couldn't get his act together; he'd sunk every last penny into getting the bakery set up, but when it finally opened, he didn't have an established customer base. And because he didn't have enough cash in savings to cover the rent during this slow period, he was doomed from the start.

Frowning, Gil shook his head and stared at Daryl with arms akimbo. "Don't do that—don't you demonize me. Daryl, the guy hadn't paid his rent in six months. I had to evict him and you know it."

"Yeah, yeah, I know," Daryl responded, waving his hand impatiently. "It just feels weird that you're here now, snatching up pieces of the guy's broken dreams."

"Sold! The range goes to Number 326 for $700!"

Gil stared wide-eyed at his friend, momentarily ignoring the auctioneer's proclamation. "That's cute. Very poetic—are you sure you're in the right line of work?" Gil jeered, but noticed a hint of genuine despondency in his friend's eyes. "Well, it's too late now... let's get outta here."

Daryl nodded, and the two of them left together.

In the parking lot—they'd been able to park next to each other—Gil slammed the back gate of his pickup closed and peered into the flatbed. Three large chalkboards, two cocktail tables, a toaster oven, an outdoor heating lamp, and a bundle of aprons met his eyes.

He pursed his lips and blew a raspberry. "I should have brought more rope. I'm probably going to avoid the freeway. You know, the aprons could just sit up front with me and..." he trailed off, noticing the still-sullen look on his friend's face.

"Hey, look, I'm sorry I brought you out here. I didn't mean to bum you out—I was just trying to help."

Daryl, who had been lost in thought, snapped out of it. "Nah, it's okay, man. Truth is, I don't even have—what was the winning bid? $700? I just don't have it. This weekend's gonna be all about me getting my hands dirty fixing that piece of crap. My wife's gonna help too—she'll be working the play button on a ton of online tutorials.

"Thanks for thinking of me and all, but this place is still a little too rich for my blood... and it's kinda depressing."

Gil chuckled. "Well, maybe to restaurant owners, but—"

Daryl held both of his hands out as if he were about to pick up a large box. "But *I'm* a restaurant owner." As he said this, he took his hands inward and pointed them to his chest. "*And* I'm your tenant. You're my landlord, Gil. I mean, Jesus, you—you sound like a sociopath. Is this supposed to be a vision of the future? How long until you're out here buying my old equipment?"

Gil looked puzzled. "Are you worried I'm not going to renew your lease? Daryl, as long as you pay your rent—"

Daryl interrupted again, which visibly peeved Gil. "See, that's the thing. The rent's not the problem... yet. But who's moving in next door, huh? A fast food restaurant? Because, if so, I got news for you pal: I'm not gonna be able to cut the mustard. My margins are already so low that even discounts aren't in the cards for me. If some chain moves in there and starts offering six hamburgers for a dollar, I'm finished."

Gil hadn't considered this. It would be nice to put a chain restaurant in there—they'd probably pay their damn rent—but Daryl was right; it would likely just put his friend out of business.

His mouth worked for a bit, then he responded, "I just want someone who will pay the bills on time, Daryl. That could be a music store, an accounting firm, or even an antique shop; it doesn't matter." Putting his arm around his friend, he donned a wry smile and added, "Besides, why would I give one deadbeat the boot just to create another?"

Daryl didn't laugh, but he did seem reassured. "Very funny."

Gil sighed. "Look. Truly, man, I'm sorry. I know what this place is and what it probably means to you, and I'm sorry for making light of it. I shouldn't be cracking jokes right now. It's just... Linda mentioned to me yesterday your gas range had gone belly up, and I knew this guy was going to be out here to auction off his stuff to try and recoup some losses. I wasn't scoping him out, though—he told me he was gonna be here tonight. I mean, he probably knew I'd wanna buy up some of his gear. And I guess I thought it would be a quick fix for you."

"It's okay, Gil. Maybe I'm a little touchy. It was just scary is all, seeing someone get evicted. We're good. But I better get going."

Gil nodded. "Yeah. I'll see you Monday." They shook hands, got in their respective cars, and drove to their respective homes.

Gil pulled into his garage and walked inside—he decided he'd unload the truck later. As he set his wallet, keys, and smartphone on a side table and turned on the lights, he scanned his surroundings and admitted to himself with some reluctance that Daryl had been right: his house did resemble a sort of hunting lodge, and the game was indeed failed startups.

But it's not like he put them all out of business; in fact, the bakery owner had the honor of being the only person he'd ever had to evict from the small strip mall he owned. Gil just... had a knack for keeping an eye on local businesses with going-out-of-business signs.

There was a tax preparation company a few miles away that always rented the same space from January to May. By June, they'd be hauling all the furniture off to the dumpster, and there would be Gil.

And when the fifth sushi restaurant on the edge of town went out of business due to lack of patronage, Gil saw deals in his eyes when a sixth sushi joint took its place. One could say it was something of a thrill for him.

He walked into his kitchen, outfitted with various bits of industrial cooking gear, and slumped his shoulders. Having all this stuff had gradually inspired him into quite a capable cook, but he just wasn't feeling it tonight; he'd struck out pretty bad trying to help a friend fix a rather serious issue.

He briefly thought about the pork that'd been marinating all day in his fridge, but ultimately marched to the pantry where he pulled out a loaf of bread and a jar of peanut butter.

Striding into his eclectic living room a few moments later with a peanut butter and jelly sandwich and a glass of milk, he flopped onto the couch that used to sit in the waiting room of a barber shop.

Folding his sandwich into something that resembled a taco, he took a gigantic bite as he turned on a flat screen TV that at one time hung in the lobby of a sports bar. A rerun of an old sitcom flickered onto the screen, and it was boring, but there wasn't really anything else on at this hour.

After finishing his sandwich and drinking most of his glass of milk, he finally started to doze off just as the family on TV began neatly wrapping up and resolving whatever ridiculous issue they'd been presented with thirty minutes prior. But with the last bit of consciousness fading away, Gil snapped back awake and touched his forehead. *Garbage night*, he remembered.

He had to walk across the street and peek at his neighbor's cans to remind himself whether it was recycling or green waste that would be picked up the next day, and then rolled his cans down to the street. Out of the corner of his eye, he spotted a neighbor about five doors down who was out for a late-night walk. Gil waved to him, and the neighbor lifted his hand to wave back before suddenly leaping into the air to an astounding height—something like twenty feet. He hovered there for a moment, eyes so wide Gil could see the whites, and then came screaming back down to the sidewalk.

Gil was stunned for a moment, but seeing the man groan and writhe in agony snapped him out of it. He started towards his neighbor at a jog. En route, a parked car between the two men reared up on its hind wheels, stood for just a moment, and then unceremoniously tipped over onto its hood. Its alarm began blaring as shattered glass spilled into the street. Face curled in confusion—he'd lost his nerve—Gil skidded to a halt and sprinted back towards his house.

As he ran past the home of his next-door neighbor, bark nuggets from the front yard rose up towards the sky. Many of them lazily slapped Gil's face as he ran through them, and then they abruptly fell to the ground. Passing the garbage cans he'd just rolled down to the street, he saw one lift slightly and slam into the other, knocking them both over and regurgitating their contents.

He made a dash up his front lawn; however, gradually coming to a stop during a full sprint, Gil looked down in a panic and discovered that his shoes no longer touched the ground. He flew to a height of nearly fifty feet, and then freefell back towards the lawn.

Screaming, and mere inches from the ground, he was jerked back up into the air at an angle, hitting the back of his head on an illuminated street lamp. As the glass of the street lamp shattered, covering his front yard in a blanket of darkness, the lights in Gil's head went out as well.

Gil coughed. He lay on his side now with vomit pooled in his cheek like a ladle. His lips curled back from his teeth, and he groaned. The vomit started to slide out, and he puckered and spat to hurry it along into the small puddle in front of his face. He could feel a warmth behind him—something near his back that was now reaching uncomfortably-high temperatures, which was in stark contrast to the freezing cold he felt over the rest of his body. His arms and legs broke out in goose bumps. He started to open his eyes, but his lids slammed shut—the overwhelming brightness was too much for his unadjusted pupils.

Where the hell am I? he wondered. He tried to retrace his steps through the night, but couldn't recall where he was or how he got there. The last thing he remembered was dozing off on his couch. *Am I dreaming?*

He pointed his face at the cold, hard floor. Shivering—it was like lying on the floor of a walk-in refrigerator—he slit one eye enough to let some of the painful light in. Underneath the smear of his partially-digested sandwich, he was able to determine he was lying on bare metal. The dark grey surface had the dull sheen of a piece of Barro

Negro pottery—meticulously polished so it was smooth to the touch, and shiny enough to produce a blurry reflection. Gil's breath was visible, and it fogged a portion of the metal he was staring at.

Slowly and stiffly, Gil picked himself up until he stood on his hands and knees. Eyes gradually adjusting to the bright light, he touched his chin to his chest and looked down the length of his body. He must have rolled the back of his head in his vomit, because it now ran up his downturned head.

He was still dressed in his faded black t-shirt with dark blue jeans and sneakers. The t-shirt displayed a Hard Rock Cafe logo with SACRAMENTO printed underneath in capital letters. He could see a small hole had been torn near the shirt's logo, but he didn't mind—he had a whole box of these shirts at home. Beyond his feet, Gil saw the source of the warmth that was on his back a moment ago: a rapidly-spinning disc, maybe five feet in diameter, an inch thick, and glowing bright orange. It hovered a little ways off the ground, emitting a low and steady hum.

Beyond the spinning disc, panels consisting of the same dark material underneath Gil extended outward and slightly upward until reaching a wall. Looking side-to-side, Gil was able to determine that he was sitting just outside the center of a large, circular room. The spinning disc must have been the exact center. The ground below it seemed to dip lower than the rest of the room—almost imperceptible, the ground seemed to be just concave enough so that water would pool in the center of the room.

He looked at his shirt again and reread the several words that decorated it. *I think I heard somewhere that you can't read while dreaming*, he thought, *so that's ruled out. So where am I?* At last, Gil lifted his head and looked in front of him, locking eyes in an instant with one of the four figures at the end of the room.

Then, Gil urinated. And indeed, it did run to the center.

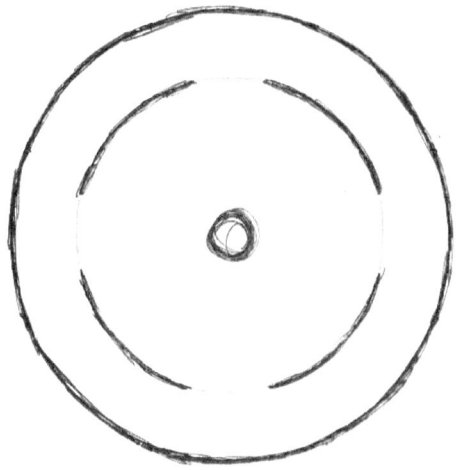

CHAPTER TWO: INTRODUCTIONS

Gil froze for a moment, stunned by the bizarre sight in front of him. It was only when the cold air in the room stung his eyes and forced him to blink that he realized he'd been holding his breath—he inhaled sharply, reinvigorating the goose bumps all over his body. He tried again to remember where he was, but the only thing that came to mind was falling asleep on his couch. It felt far too real to be a dream, and he wondered if he'd been taken from his home while he slept. He felt scared, but as he got to his feet, his initial terror dissipated. His heavy breathing quieted and he started to calm down—no one was running towards him or even moving at all. He squinted and exhaled, cocking his head to one side. Now he was just annoyed.

Despite what was standing in front of him, a dozen feet away behind the clearest sheet of glass he'd ever laid eyes on, Gil didn't have a doubt in his mind that this was all bogus. It had to be a setup—an elaborate prank concocted by some group of jerks with a camera. Maybe one of those stupid reality TV shows where they scoop up some sap and try to scare the crap out of him for laughs—and he'd already pissed himself.

The dead giveaway, as far as Gil was concerned, was the stillness of it all—it was like looking into a museum diorama. At one end of the large and round room he stood in, the sheet of glass separated Gil from four beings that looked like what he supposed space aliens would look like. He had never really thought about what a space alien or the inside of an alien ship might look like before now, but as a child of the 90s, he had seen his fair share of science fiction movies and these four things fit the bill pretty damn well.

One of them was very short, like a middle-school child. Two others were a bit taller, and behind them was a fourth alien that towered above at what had to be about seven feet—tall by any standard, but a giant compared to its friends. Each pair of disproportionately-large, black, and shiny eyes was housed in a body that otherwise looked powder-white and featureless. They looked fleshy but rail-thin, completely hairless, and inexplicably naked. Two thin and diagonal lines, barely visible from the distance Gil saw them, made up a nose. There were no visible ears or mouths, but the heads were shaped as if to accommodate them—a prominent chin under the faint nose, and concave indents where he expected ears would be.

They each had a slender torso with arms and legs like sticks. His eyesight wasn't awesome at this distance, but they appeared to have five long fingers on each hand. Focusing on one of the torsos, he saw a clearly-defined chest, but no nipples. Farther down, there was no belly button. And even farther down, there was... absolutely nothing. Gil scoffed and chalked this up to lazy design. They were run-of-the-mill "Greys," the generic alien design Gil had seen in everything from *South Park* to *The X-Files*. The only difference, Gil noticed, was that the color was wrong—they were called Greys for a reason, but these things weren't grey at all.

The beings were also completely lifeless. *Just props*, Gil thought, and sighed again. Of course he thought they were staring at him. Their eyes were so damn big they'd have to do a one-eighty for Gil to feel like they *weren't* staring at him—like a statue in a haunted house, they were likely designed to appear as if their gaze followed the viewer in passing. He assured himself again they were clearly fake—not even any signs of breathing. Gil figured that if he'd woken up in his bed in the middle of the night with one of these things standing in the darkness, he'd have had a massive heart attack and died right then and there—they'd never be able to air that on television. But in this bright light, they just looked... hokey.

He took in his surroundings, and he admitted they were elaborate for a fake—maybe it was an old movie prop? The surface area of the ground, walls, and ceiling all shared the same, roughly-polished hematite finish. Behind the glass pane on the edge of the round room— past the dummies—elaborate piping weaved in and out of a planked wall, terminating at various points with strange vents, meters, and turn valves. They were all normal enough for Gil to understand what they were, but their aesthetics were still unfamiliar.

Above him, various channels in the ceiling fed light into the large room. The sides of each channel obscured the source of the recessed light, but it was bright enough to spill over and reflect off all of the room's polished surfaces. Gil turned around and looked up. The channels all led to the center of the room, where they met and formed a circle around a large disc—a metallic circle with a lighter finish than the rest of the room. It reminded him of brushed nickel.

This of course put it directly above the spinning disc that hovered off the ground, but unlike the flat surface of its counterpart, the disc on the ceiling had a series of odd stalactites hanging from it. Not natural, and perfectly smooth, but cave stalactites was the closest thing he could compare it to. There were dozens of them, at various lengths, all pointing straight down. The orange glow from the disc near the ground reflected off of it brilliantly, and—

Gil's train of thought was interrupted by an abrupt and loud bang on the window behind him. He whirled around, heart pounding in his chest, and looked back at the four figures. The three shorter figures were situated just as he remembered them. But the taller one—the giant—was no longer standing straight up with its arms at its sides. Its left arm was now raised with its hand open and pressed against the glass. Its eyes now seemed to be arched down in anger, and its neck was extended to bring the head closer to the window.

Gil, who was on the verge of pissing himself again, thought of a creepy wax museum—he'd never been to a wax museum he didn't find at least a little creepy, but he especially disliked the type that moved. He saw no seams or joints on the dummies to allow rotation, though Gil imagined it would be easy enough to swap one static wax figure out for another.

Were there a dozen wax figures hiding just out of the view of the window? Did some zit-faced little stage tech come out from stage left and swap props while he had his back turned? Gil didn't like to be scared, and he thought he might like to punch that intern right in the nose, but the feeling quickly evaporated: while Gil's eyes were fixed on the giant, it drew back its hand, balled it into a fist, and slammed it again into the window. It moved its head even closer, stretching its neck out and fogging the window with its breath. Gil gasped, cupped his hands over his mouth, and let loose a string of profanity. He watched it happen. No stage tech in sight; this was not a television show, and that thing just goddamn moved.

The giant once again drew its arm back before pivoting its feet smoothly to the left. It marched past the view of the window and out of sight, but Gil could hear it walking along the outside of the round room. Its enormous footfalls made it easy for Gil's bulging eyes to follow it. As thin as the being was, it would have to be incredibly dense for its feet to hit the ground that hard.

Ninety degrees to the left of the window—exactly where Gil's head had swiveled to—a panel recessed and then slid to the right behind the adjacent section of wall. Another brilliantly-clear glass sheet was revealed with the giant standing behind it, and no sooner than the panel moved out of the way did the glass sheet do the same thing in the opposite direction. There was now nothing between them.

The giant stomped towards Gil and stopped in front of him, hairless eyebrows arching more and appearing even angrier than before. A small and weak, "Oh my God," escaped Gil's mouth, in a quick exhale that made it sound like just a single syllable. The words left him along with any last shreds of doubt about the creature.

He couldn't believe he ever thought this behemoth was a fake; now that it was in front of him, Gil observed a heart beating visibly in a chest that subtly rose and fell with each breath. Further, though still closed, it was obvious that this thing did indeed have a mouth—a low-toned and barely audible growl escaped from the slit it hid behind. The exhalation steamed in the cold room.

Gil did not dare reach out and touch it, but its skin looked to have the texture of sun-bleached driftwood—rough and porous. Worse, the thing stank—it stank like old fish and body odor. It made him gag for a moment, but fear of how the alien might react to his vomit forced him to hold it in. His mouth clapped shut, teeth clenching like a vice grip to hold back the retching and rendering him powerless to avoid breathing in the stench. He rapidly inhaled and exhaled though his nose like a wailing infant who'd only just been given a bottle.

He looked down and took in the rest of the strange creature. Its tall and thin legs were interrupted halfway down by a pair of knobby knees, and ended in two thin feet—mostly familiar in shape, but with only three toes, and no toenails. The entire surface of its body was utterly devoid of wrinkles, birth marks, scarring, or, really, anything. The only exception was when skin was forced to overlap itself and form crow's feet, such as the joints of its armpits, or the corners of its eyes.

The alien leaned in closer and towered its head over Gil, who instinctively looked up and met the alien's gaze. And once he got a good look at its eyes, he couldn't look away.

From a distance, Gil had seen only two massive, black, and featureless orbs within the head of each alien. But with the giant's eyes now just inches away from his own, an overwhelming amount of detail came into focus that forced a pained whine from deep within Gil's gut. They were huge, and they terrified him. Everything that made up a human eye—a sclera, an iris, a pupil—seemed to be present here, but they were all different shades of black that became only barely visible when penetrated by the light. The glow of the room refracted in its eyes like jet-black polished quartz, and Gil felt as if he were falling into those seemingly bottomless pupils. He became lightheaded and his intestines seemed to rise up into his chest, as if he were plummeting from a great height. Gil began to babble.

His words disintegrated as they fell out of his mouth. Questions of what was happening and pleas to be taken away from this place mixed together and resulted in an incoherent mess of words. As much as he wanted to, Gil couldn't break eye contact with the giant. He stared helplessly into its eyes, the massive irises contracting as the alien's focus intensified.

Suddenly, the giant's head snapped to Gil's right, and it stared back at the other three beings. The break in eye contact felt like a hand loosening around Gil's neck. Catching his breath somewhat, Gil was reminded of the stench and tried hard to control his breathing. He looked to his right as well, where he saw that the three shorter beings stood exactly as they had when Gil had first laid eyes on them. His confused gaze shifted back and forth between the beings at the far end of the room and the goliath in front of him, wondering what was going on. The taller alien turned to once again face Gil, quickly stepped around to his other side, and wrapped its left hand around the back of Gil's neck. Hot enough to make him sweat, the hand grabbing him felt like dried-up driftwood, sun-bleached and baking in the sun. He yelped in pain as the alien angrily pushed forward and marched them both towards the three shorter beings.

Gil fought hard to keep up, all the while protesting and begging to stop. He spent most of the short trip unable to keep in step with the giant's long strides and found himself seamlessly dragged when he slipped—the strength of the being was immense. As the two of them approached the window, Gil was gradually lowered until his knees banged against the ground. He became aware that their pace was not changing. He screamed, pleading to slow down or stop entirely, and then snapped his eyes shut and clenched his teeth to brace himself.

A pained grunt erupted from Gil as his forward motion halted abruptly—his face had just smashed nose-first into the large window. Vision blurry, and with his knees brushing against the floor, he muttered idle threats through a slack jaw as the giant used the palm of its free hand to push back on Gil's forehead.

Basically on his knees, the hand forced him to look upwards at the three beings, which all still remained completely... actually, now that Gil was this close, he saw the same familiar signs of life observed in their taller friend. And... had their heads all angled down slightly to meet his gaze?

Frightened and exhausted, Gil obeyed and stared at the beings for a long while before finally shouting, "What! What do you want?!" He didn't know what else to say—what else to ask. He just didn't know what they wanted, and they didn't seem to be keen on telling him. In fact they hadn't said a word—could they even speak? And why the hostility? He didn't poke his head in through the front door of wherever this was and ask if he could come in. He wasn't some door-to-door salesman peddling magazine subscriptions. No, they had brought him to wherever this was, and were now treating him like a peasant in the presence of royalty. If the giant was anything to go by, Gil's presence alone was offensive.

The beings stood and stared blankly at Gil as if he'd been quiet as a mouse, and then suddenly, perhaps independent of Gil's intense questioning, their eyes grew wide. They seemed awe-struck, filled with wonder.

The alien farthest from Gil reached up and touched something near the edge of the window—some sort of button or panel—causing the sheet of glass to slide away and disappear into the wall. It and another of the beings turned to Gil's left and ran down the corridor.

Their footfalls, though nowhere near as massive as their taller companion, were still disconcertingly heavy. The remaining short alien—the shortest, actually—approached Gil slowly and studied his face. Gil averted his blurry gaze, making up his mind that he never wanted to get a good look at their eyes again.

The two short aliens returned moments later, one of them holding a thin, uncapped vial. They were all crowded around Gil now. Even the tallest being, who still had one hand wrapped around the back of Gil's neck with the other pressed against his forehead, looked on in amazement.

The smack on the front of Gil's face had of course been painful, but it was dwarfed by the incredible discomfort of the position the tall alien continued to hold him in. It was as if it had been meant as a cue for Gil to regard the aliens in some way, like a father chastising a child for ignoring a mother's inquiries.

Gil was just high enough off the ground that his knees could feel the cold metal, but not close enough that he could rest his weight on it—nearly all of his weight rested on the hand wrapped around his neck, and as a result, he felt like an old-time circus performer who'd had the awful luck of a lion biting down directly on his head. With some effort, his feet scrambled underneath himself until he finally stood in a squatting position. He was at last supporting some of his weight.

One of the aliens shoved the vial underneath Gil's nose with a noticeable lack of grace. It made an airtight seal with his nostril, which Gil realized meant he must have been bleeding from the nose—his blood had formed a gasket. Gil stared back at the aliens in similar amazement. Did they not bleed themselves? If they did, how could they possibly be so shocked that smashing his face into a window would result in a nosebleed?

After a few moments, the alien holding the vial drew its hand back and looked at the now-brimming sample of blood. Given how quickly the vial had filled, Gil thought there must have been a small pool of blood on the floor—it likely accounted for some of the difficulty in getting his feet stabilized.

The alien holding the vial rotated its hand to look at its index finger—some of Gil's blood had spilled from the brim and now rested in a fat droplet near its fingertip. The other two aliens Gil could see followed suit and stared at the droplet, and after a moment, it was absorbed into the alien's skin like water disappearing into a pumice stone. Gil couldn't be sure—though too scared to openly cry, his vision was still blurry with tears—but for just an instant, he could have sworn the point of absorption turned slightly grey.

The vial was capped and quickly set aside. The alien held up the affected hand with its index finger pointed upward, and the other two gathered around, all examining the finger with intense curiosity.

Gil, still staring in sheer bewilderment, hadn't realized that the blood running from his nose had begun to pool in his gaping mouth. The taste of iron finally clued him in just as a single drop of it aspirated into his lungs. Gil snapped his mouth shut, but couldn't keep himself from coughing—the blood in his mouth ejected in a viscous spray that showered the aliens in a pink mist. The collective scream that resulted made Gil shudder.

The giant drew both its hands away from Gil in an instant, sending him sprawling towards the floor. Gil stared at the ground, too terrified to look up, but he could hear them stomping around in a panic. The commotion gradually dwindled, the blood likely disappearing into their skin, but Gil continued to stare down, now lost in thought.

He wondered just what the hell these things were—could the sandpapery feeling of the giant's skin be attributed to a lack of moisture? On one of the little guys, its finger had consumed Gil's blood like an open mouth. He pictured white driftwood again, but that wasn't right... the skin felt hard and thick, but also flexible. It was the roughest, thickest, most calloused skin Gil had ever felt—and so hot! From his low vantage point, he saw steamy condensation forming on the ground along the outlines of their feet and figured that if he were that warm, he'd have a fever intense enough to cause brain damage.

The giant balled up its fist and punched the wall. Gil's focus jolted upwards, but he realized that he wasn't the target of its rage—it was staring at its shorter travel companions in an expression that seemed almost like defiance. Again, the fist collided with the wall, and its foot stomped in protest. It looked like a tantrum.

After a few tense moments, its eyes suddenly dropped back down to look at Gil. And of course, Gil looked down so as to not make eye contact. He could feel it step behind him. The giant shoved its hands underneath his armpits, and hoisted him to his feet in a single, smooth motion. Pushing Gil along like a hostage, all five of them exited the large room.

Craning his neck around, Gil saw the doorway behind them disappear—the sheet of glass slid back into place, and a darkly metallic panel slid from the opposite direction, clicking as it came to a stop and blending in with the rest of the wall. It was as if a doorway had never been there.

The five of them moved down the left of the dimly-lit corridor that wrapped around the circular room they'd just exited. To his right, Gil saw that the wall opposite the round room was made up entirely of roughly eight-inch-wide vertical planks, one after another, only interrupted by a small porthole every twenty-or-so feet. In passing, he looked through the first porthole he could get his eyes on, but saw only darkness.

They all halted abruptly at a porthole seemingly identical to the others. The shortest alien raised a hand and pressed one of its slender fingers to the wall underneath the porthole. A glowing symbol appeared underneath its finger, which then swiped downward. The planks collapsed under each other, contracting to the left and right from the location of the plank the alien had interacted with.

It revealed a room wider than it was deep. The ceiling at the far end of the room tapered off, dipping so low at the wall that Gil wouldn't be able to walk all the way to the end of the room without bonking his head on the ceiling.

The three short aliens walked inside, and the tall one resumed shoving Gil along. Looking up into the room, Gil spotted an exam table and instinctively planted his feet to the floor, shifting his weight against the pushy alien. He felt pretty sure he wouldn't like anything that might happen in here, and a quick mental scan of all the extraterrestrial movies he'd seen told him he had good reason to want to opt out of whatever they had planned for him.

But the thing pushing him was stronger—*much* stronger—than Gil, and it didn't falter. The other three stood around the exam table, waiting for Gil to be delivered so they could get to work.

A fresh fear washed over Gil as he approached. The last thing he needed after his introduction to these four assholes was for them to start drilling holes in his teeth and shoving stuff up his ass. Those procedures would be nightmarish even if conducted by the world's best dentist and proctologist, but these bozos? He got the feeling pain wasn't a concept these things were familiar with and doubted they were about to break out the kid gloves now.

The big alien picked Gil up and deposited him onto the table despite loud and damning protests. He called them perverts. He threatened them. He begged them to stop and take him home. But they carried on as if he hadn't said a word. One of the shorter beings pulled his shirt up to his armpits while the tall one pinned his arms down.

In his efforts to avoid making eye contact with any of them, Gil turned his head to the left. Past one of the beings, he saw something resembling a long oven—or rather, a wide oven. Ashes were scattered around the floor of it in little piles and, realizing he'd fit in there rather nicely, Gil looked to his right. Next to another one of the beings, a thin rod protruded from the ground and terminated in a large bulb. And jutting out of the bulb were various scalpels, spikes, and serrated blades.

Gil, still shouting and with nothing comforting to look at, shut his eyes tightly and braced himself for the worst.

And then, suddenly, the pressure on his arms lifted. Gil opened his eyes and saw the tall one was walking away; it took a seat next to the entrance of the room and continued to conspicuously stare at Gil with what looked to him like resentment. He couldn't be sure if it was resentment, but that downward-arched brow seemed like a good indication.

One of the shorter ones—he couldn't keep track of which was which—dipped its hand into the rear of the bulb and scooped out a small handful of clear, viscous paste. Then its hand hovered over Gil's head and torso, stopping every now and again to dab a tiny amount on his skin. As it did this, another of the aliens produced a number of black wires, and it stuck one into each of the dabs of paste. When they were both finished, it resembled a hospital EKG unit. They walked away, joining the other short one at a nearby counter outfitted with various assembled technologies.

With the tall one still sulking near the entrance, Gil nervously watched the other three as they did... whatever it was they were doing. He couldn't help but notice that all three of them had dark, dry mud on the upper portions of their backs; from shoulder to shoulder, each wore a dry and cracked smear of something that resembled a mudpack.

Gil thought the smallest of them looked almost childlike. Unlike the almond-shaped eyes the rest of them wore, this short alien's eyes looked almost round by comparison, bright with what appeared to Gil as enthusiasm and confidence. It also looked to be the busiest, executing various swiping gestures on touch screens and inputting data.

Behind it, one of the midsized aliens stood with its arms crossed as if supervising, but the expression of what seemed like confusion indicated that it just wasn't sure what was going on or how to contribute. The other of the midsized aliens sat next to the short one and also stared, but looked to be paying close and knowing attention to the display in front of them.

Meanwhile, for nearly ten minutes after being equipped with their otherworldly EKG, Gil rested on his back with his head on its side so he could see them. He occasionally glanced back over to the tall alien to see if its stare persisted, and it always did. Just once, Gil started to hesitantly get up, but lost his nerve when the giant snapped to its feet. It clearly wanted him to stay put.

Turning his attention back to the counter and its perplexing components, he could see they were obviously monitoring his vitals, but he wasn't sure for what purpose. Also, the vial of blood they'd collected from his nosebleed was hooked up to some sort of device—perhaps for some sort of analysis, but again, he couldn't be sure.

Gil didn't know a whole lot about blood, but he'd donated a pint here and there and had made a couple of observations. First, and the most obvious, was that it was usually drawn from a vein. As far as he knew, technicians didn't make a habit of bopping people on the nose and hanging their heads over a funnel.

But perhaps more importantly, great care had always been taken to seal the blood off from any contaminants and store it at a controlled temperature. Never mind the sweat and snot swimming around in there, the vial likely wasn't sterilized to begin with.

Seemingly on cue, one of them let out an agitated grunt, ripped the vial from the device, and poured it into something that looked like a small sink—the sample had been unusable. Then another one of them, the one who previously stood with its arms crossed, walked over to where Gil lay. When it reached the table, it grabbed one of Gil's ankles and harshly yanked him half-way off. He shrieked as the wires attached to him tore free, bringing with them the now-solidified dabs of paste, plus patches of Gil's hair and skin.

Gil kept himself from slipping off the table by gripping the edge of it with his hands and digging his fingers into the underside. The abrupt halt forced him into a seated position, and he was now face-to-face with the agitated alien. Standing, Gil would have been taller by about a foot; but on this short table, where his feet touched the ground, the alien actually had an inch or two on him. Its stench made Gil lightheaded. And then the alien drew closer, examining Gil's nose. He could see the individual pores in its skin, like pinholes in white clay. Its eyes narrowed, and then its warm thumb and index finger pinched Gil's nose shut, as if to turn it like a spigot. Gil grimaced and moaned in discomfort.

"What are you..." Gil began, but stopped when the alien took advantage of his open mouth and shoved its fingers inside. The clump of fingers pried his mouth open wide and moved his tongue back and forth. Gil wretched at the taste, like dirty pennies with a dusting of salt, and shouted. He finally lifted both hands, pushed the alien away, and then spat several times onto the floor. The foul taste in his mouth persisted.

"God, what's the matter with you?" Gil shouted. When he looked up again, still grimacing, he saw the tall one near the edge of the room had gotten up and was now heading towards him. In front of him, one of the other aliens headed his way with what looked like a cross between a syringe and a pistol in its right hand. The barrel consisted of an incredibly-thick needle, and the gun's cylinder was a glass tube. It held its hand around the grip with its index finger on a long and curved trigger.

Gil panicked and flailed his arms to keep them away. Just as the tall one reached him, and completely by accident, Gil's hand made contact with the giant's eye like one might grab a bowling ball. It was unpleasant for both of them.

The giant grunted loudly before grabbing Gil's flailing arm with its left hand and viciously backhanding him with its right. This got Gil's nose bleeding again, but his captors no longer seemed interested. The one holding the syringe dropped it onto the floor and then aggressively pushed the giant back. For a moment, Gil only had a vague idea of the fight that broke out behind him as he wormed his way between them and scurried to the corridor. At least two of them were grunting and barking over the sounds of footfalls and closed fists colliding with their thin frames.

Gil turned around and was shocked to see that he was right—the tall one and one of the others were engaged in some sort of fistfight, while the other two attempted to intervene and separate them. *What the hell is going on?* he wondered. After some more struggling, the tallest alien stumbled backwards and bumped into Gil, who then also stumbled backwards, tripped over his own feet, and fell onto his rear end right inside the center room. The giant whipped around, deciding to direct its anger back to Gil, but then the shortest of them ran to the doorway and tapped at something off to the side. Gil stared up at them and saw that they were now all standing at the threshold. One of them had wrapped a hand around the upper arm of the giant in an attempt to hold it in place. They stared as the glass pane slid shut, and as soon as it clicked into place, a panel revealed itself and closed over the window. He heard footsteps outside the room disperse and slowly fade away.

Now, all the walls in the large room looked exactly the same: a ring of identical, dull, and dark silver panels. Gil would have to look at his cold smear of vomit or the now-congealed pool of blood to be able to determine where the first door had been. Then the room went dark—pitch black at first, but eventually a dull orange color as Gil's eyes adjusted. The spinning disc from the center of the area finally had the floor to itself, and its dull glow touched everything in the room.

Gil put his hands behind him and slowly lowered himself onto his back, breathing hard with eyes wide open. Now alone with his thoughts, and with his situation settling in his mind, his new terror was the possibility of a heart attack. He forced his eyes shut and whispered, reciting basic facts about himself. "Deep breaths," he said aloud. "Just take deep breaths." Each time a flash of the exam materialized in his mind, his heartbeat quickened, so Gil told himself he had to let it go for now and just focus on not dying. And, eventually, his breathing did slow down. He sat for a long time, with measured inhales and slow exhales. At last, he opened his eyes again.

The orange glow seemed surprisingly bright now. Gil slowly made his way to his feet, with growing awareness of the immense pain he was in. He felt as if he'd spent an hour in a tumble dryer after the ordeal with those strange creatures, and the cold temperature of his surroundings didn't help. He paced around the room for a short time as his mind raced. He tried, but failed to verbalize his current situation. He could hardly think it, let alone say it out loud. And before long, he found that he could hardly think at all—Gil was exhausted.

On the verge of shivering, Gil looked to the center of the room. He remembered that the spinning disc was uncomfortably warm, and now its delicious heat beckoned to him. En route to the center of the room, Gil wondered whether or not it was safe—the thing might be radioactive, and a nap too close to it meant that Gil could wake up with all manner of ailments that would make his hosts seem like resort masseuses by comparison. But his pace didn't falter—he reached the disc, curled up into a fetal position, and as the dubious heat warmed his back, sleep overtook him.

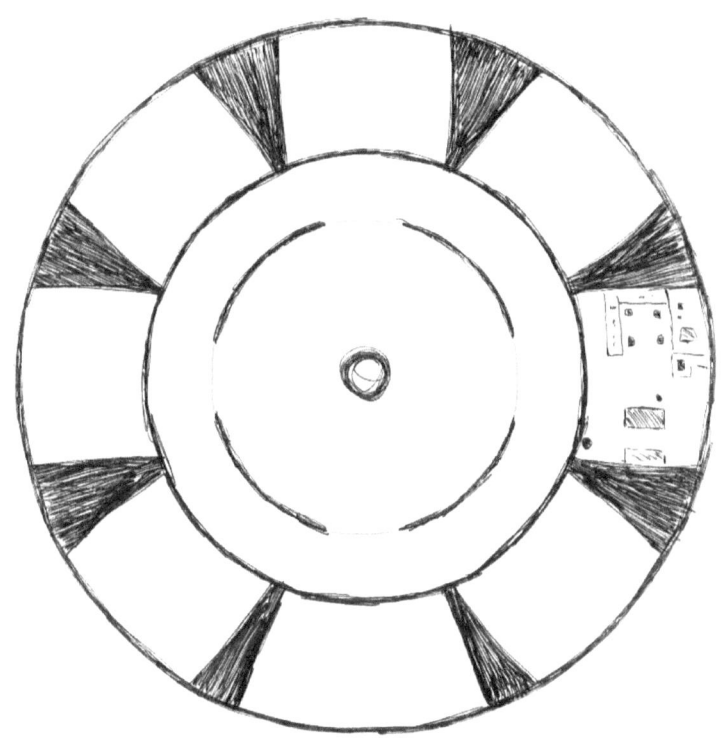

CHAPTER THREE: THE NAMING CEREMONY

Gil awoke from dreamless sleep some time later on his side, face resting on his hands. The lights flickered to life again. He was still tired, still dirty, and now thirsty to boot. His stomach growled and he thought he also wouldn't mind something to eat. Touching the tips of his fingers to his cheeks, he felt the sandpapery roughness of a day's stubble.

Facing the disc—he must have rolled over in his sleep—he wondered what would happen if he were to touch it. Would it burn him? Electrocute him? Would it feel like sticking his finger into a spinning fan? Suppose it wasn't actually spinning at all? He didn't have the nerve to find out; he rolled back over onto his other side and found himself, once again, a room's length away from the four aliens.

Just as before, they separated themselves from Gil with a sheet of clear glass. But this time, the corridor gave way to a sort of kitchen area, where they were seated and didn't seem to be paying close attention to him. Instead, they were focused on small meals. The look of the aliens set Gil's teeth on edge. *So ugly,* he thought. His mouth worked for a moment, until he finally asked in a voice barely qualifying as a whisper, "Why am I still here?" He was only just beginning to come to terms with where he was and what he was a part of. But he'd expected the encounter to be done by now.

He sat up and looked around. The remnants of his vomit were behind him, which meant this window was on the opposite side of the room from where he first encountered them.

The aliens sat at a round table surrounded with eight backless chairs protruding like stumps from the ground. Every surface, including the table and chairs, had the same, now-familiar dark grey metal finish. It was also seamless, as if the table and chairs had bloomed from the ground like blown glass. In front of each of them was a small white plate topped with pink cubes.

They ate with their bare fingers, pinching one cube at a time and delicately inserting it into seemingly lipless mouths. They chewed openly, teeth bared, sickly grey tongue massaging pink mush. They also each had a tall, white, tubular pipe next to their plates with a tapered edge like the end of a woodwind instrument. They were drinking glasses. Whatever they were drinking, Gil figured the edge probably made insertion into their tight mouths more manageable.

Gil stood up and slowly walked towards the glass. The four figures shot him an absent glance, and then went about their business. He arched his eyebrows in confusion. *That's it?* he thought, and then whispered, "Hello?" There was no response, but of course, how could anyone hear a faint whisper through a sheet of thick glass? He awkwardly shook his head and then greeted them in a loud and clear voice: "Hello?" Two of them apparently heard this and shot him another quick glance, but that was all. *What the hell is going on?* he wondered, then shouted, "Why am I still here?" He studied their faces.

There was no talking, but eyes darted around amongst them as if to suggest conversation. Gil could see now the pink cubes resembled tuna sashimi from an upscale Japanese restaurant, and the sight of it made his belly rumble. He hadn't eaten anything since his small dinner the night before—or at least it felt like it was no more than a dozen hours ago—and he'd thrown that up not far from where he stood now. He placed one hand on the glass window and the other over his stomach. After a few moments spent gawking, the tall being took notice, got up, and walked out of sight. It returned a moment later with a fresh plate and glass, and stood in front of the window.

Gil stared at the plate of food for a moment and then, after a pregnant pause, the giant took a short step back with its left foot and then kicked the window with its right. A loud thud reverberated. Gil retreated back to the center of the room and looked up with just enough time to see only the far edge of its angry face turn out of sight as it faced the others. Its back and neck muscles seemed to tense up, and then relax. After another long pause, the giant made a conspicuously-long turn back around to face Gil. The window slid open, the giant gingerly set the plate and glass down beyond the threshold, and the window returned to its closed position. The giant then returned to the table, took its seat, and resumed eating.

Gil apprehensively approached the dishes, picked them up, and returned to the warmth of the spinning disc before sitting cross-legged and setting the plate in his lap. He didn't exactly have an appetite for raw fish to begin with, but after closer examination and a few smell tests, Gil concluded that this was actually raw beef. Or, at least, that's what it looked and smelled like. He supposed it could be just about any damn thing from just about anywhere in the universe.

He briefly considered refusing it, but then remembered that he was aboard a space ship where dying at the hands of his captors was a distinct possibility. If not them, perhaps it would be the radiation poisoning he'd surely receive from sitting next to this mystery disc. With these terrifying possibilities in mind, death by food poisoning at least seemed terrestrial. Gil dug into his mystery meat. As he ate—first hesitantly, then greedily—he observed his captors.

Just who the hell are these guys, Gil thought, *and what do they want with me? More importantly, why am I just sitting around? I've heard about abductions before, sure, but they've ranged from encounters where people walk away enlightened, to horrible encounters where people have awful things shoved up their asses before being dropped back on earth with an ID tag. This, however, seems like a hostage situation perpetrated by children. I've seen the big one throw a couple of tantrums, and if the surprise at my bloody nose is any indication, they don't know anything about human anatomy. For God's sake, one of these bozos dug around in my mouth trying to find... what, a blood source? On the other hand, the one with the syringe last night might have intended to attempt a blood draw.*

Looking around the table, Gil studied the beings and tried to get a handle on their personalities. To an extent, some character traits were apparent from the start—especially with the big guy. Its elbows rested on the table, back slumped over like a thug in a seedy bar. Gil found its personality easy to peg, and he summed it up with a single word: angry. He had a feeling that, while none of them seemed to like him very much, he'd already be dead if it were just the big guy running the show.

Gil lifted the glass he'd been given and smelled the liquid. *How about that*, he thought, *it's just water*. He upturned the glass and drank its contents in a single go. Then, without any clue as to how long he'd be here, or if he was ever going to leave, Gil figured he'd better come up with a better way to identify them than, "the tall one and the other three." He decided he would give them names.

Starting with the tall one, Gil recalled a Bruce Willis movie he'd seen years ago, which featured a race of large, brown, grumpy, and war-hungry aliens called... well, actually, he couldn't remember—overall, they played a bit part. He absently reached for his hip pocket to look it up on his smartphone, then smiled and rolled his eyes. His pockets were empty. He wondered for a moment if they had taken his stuff, but a memory flickered in his mind of him dropping off his wallet, keys, and phone when he came in from his garage. Then again, if he'd had the phone with him, he would have forgotten about the stupid movie and called for help. But he didn't, so he wouldn't be looking up anything on his phone. The name of the main character from that movie stood out in his head, however, so he settled for that and decided to refer to the tall alien as Korben from now on.

To Korben's left sat the shortest of the bunch, who barely came up to Gil's elbow. In between bites of food, it timidly flicked its gaze back and forth between Korben and the other two aliens with a strange expression of optimism—as if assuring them they'd all figure out what they were supposed to be doing. This was the one who'd apparently been doing all the work in the exam room. This was also the alien who quickly shut the door after Gil's exam to put up a wall between him and Korben. There was a cartoon Gil used to watch, set far in the future, which featured many alien characters alongside humans. Looking at this being, a timid, green alien rose to the forefront of Gil's mind, and so he decided its name would be Kif.

To Kif's left sat an alien who was a bit taller but still a full head shorter than Gil. It had finished its meal, and now sat rigidly in its seat with a blank expression. It was clear at this point verbal communication wasn't how these things operated. Gil supposed it had to be telepathy or something, although even that didn't seem to align with any of the alleged abduction stories he'd heard, nor any of the science fiction movies he'd ever seen. He was thankful he hadn't been subjected to the clichéd headache induced by high-pitched wailing, but he also certainly hadn't been imparted any of the clichéd wisdom of beings from another world.

Whatever the method they used to communicate, Gil couldn't participate. *But how could they not have known that?* he wondered. *They stared at me when I first met them for what felt like ten minutes, probably trying to talk to me before Korben got impatient. As if I was being rude or something—like I was purposefully ignoring them. Did they expect me to be telepathic? What could they have so calmly been trying to tell me before Korben flew off the handle?*

But also, regardless of how they communicated, it was obvious to Gil that this third alien simply wasn't interested in participating. This was the same alien who'd collected Gil's blood and unwittingly absorbed some of it into its finger. It was also the idiot who shoved its disgusting fingers into Gil's mouth looking for blood. Now it sat like a teenager still relegated to the kids' table for the holidays. Gil decided its name had to be Jeltz.

Finally, to Jeltz's left and at around the same height sat the fourth alien. The only thing Gil had gotten from this alien was the possible intent to prick him with a big needle, and he found it difficult to name it based on that single interaction. *Or,* Gil wondered, *wasn't that also the one who stepped in when Korben backhanded me?* The name Roger came to mind, given to a particularly crass alien character from an equally crass cartoon he used to watch. The name didn't fit at all—he seriously doubted this one would have an affinity for costumes and pecan sandies—but he was running out of fictional aliens to name these creatures after.

Gil thought for a few more moments, and then his train of thought was interrupted when the pompous-looking one, Jeltz, suddenly tipped forward and smacked its face on its empty plate. It looked to have passed out. The other three aliens jumped to their feet and rushed to Jeltz's side. Korben lifted the unconscious alien upward and held its shoulders upright as red-tinged juice from the plate dripped from Jeltz's face. Its mouth hung open, huge eyelids fluttering open and shut. Then the alien came to after a few moments and gestured to the others to move away. They took their seats again, and Jeltz wiped the pink drops from its face with its hands. Before long, it was as if nothing had happened.

What the hell was that? Gil wondered. *He was fine just a minute ago.* The other three aliens stared at Jeltz with what looked like concern as they ate their meals. Gil stared at all four of them, wondering what they might be saying to each other. Was something wrong with Jeltz?

He had only just gone back to thinking about names again when the four of them rose up with their plates and walked out of view. Gil figured they'd finished their meals and were likely headed for the window afterwards. Though he was unhappy with the name, he decided Roger would have to do for the final alien.

They walked into the corridor. The kitchen area behind them disappeared as planks from the left and the right—all the same dark grey metal— obscured it like a sliding lens cover. All that remained behind them was a small, round porthole.

Gil felt good. As long as he didn't go spitting blood on them or punching any of them in the eye anymore, he'd probably be fine.

Further, it was nice to have at least a small amount of food in his belly, and it was therapeutic to sit quietly and assign identities to these strange creatures. He smiled a little—this was like Jane Goodall naming the apes she studied, but in reverse. Now in front of him, they stood silently and stared. Gil still didn't have the nerve to look any of them in the eye, but he did offer up a single, calm sentence:

"I don't know if any of you are trying to talk to me, but if you are, you gotta know that I'm not getting anything."

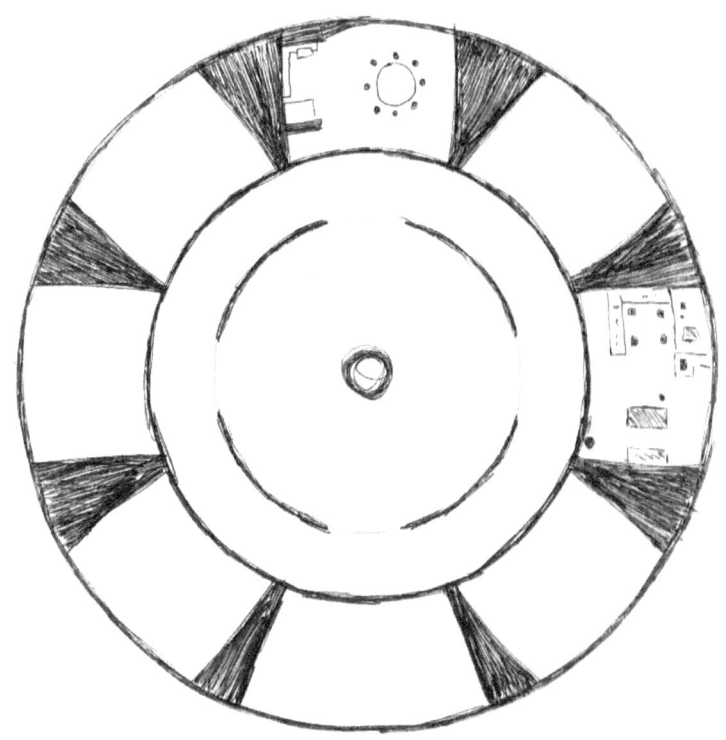

CHAPTER FOUR: SHOTS IN THE DARK

Korben, Kif, Jeltz, and Roger stood before Gil and seemed to agree that, no, he couldn't receive any of their silent transmissions. After a short period of silence, during which Gil was again reminded of their stench—it had a habit of coming back stronger than ever just as soon as he forgot about it—Kif raised a hand and pointed to the exit. Gil's eyes grew wide with surprise, as this was the first time any of them made a noticeable effort to communicate with him. "Hand gestures!" he exclaimed. He stood up and followed them.

As the five of them marched through the corridor that wrapped around the circular room, Gil looked around to try and get a sense of where things were. He knew a kitchen of sorts sat behind one of the portholes, and he'd previously seen an exam room behind another. He looked through the first porthole past the kitchen and saw a row of what he thought looked like four beds.

Gil deduced that there was likely a room behind each porthole—the setup reminded him of a large cog. The room he'd been in was the center, and the outer wall of this corridor led to the cog's many teeth. Short of observing the rooms through their small portholes, Gil saw no simple means of identifying them—they all looked the same from inside the corridor.

The others knew where they were going, however; they halted at the next porthole they reached and stared at it. Kif expanded the walls to reveal the same exam room from before. Trying to keep his cool this time, Gil proceeded agreeably. He did a little bit of mental math and quickly deduced that eight portholes would be found in the corridor, meaning eight different rooms—this particular cog had eight teeth.

Gil approached the table and willingly put his back on it. But this time, black straps were produced and pulled from the edges of the table. Two of the aliens wrapped the straps over him and attached them to the opposite ends of the table, securing his wrists, ankles, torso, and head in place. And after a brief moment of contemplation, Gil's good feeling was gone. Korben took a seat at the entrance to the room.

Jeltz stood near Gil's head and began doing things that would best be described as uncomfortable. It opened his mouth and retrieved a sample of saliva—not with a swab, but something that scraped gently along the inside of Gil's cheek. His eye was stretched open wide, and Jeltz stared into it before swabbing some of its moisture away. Gil was thankful that, despite the brightness in the room, its eyes just looked like black orbs. Something that did feel like a swab was shoved into and spun within Gil's ear. Jeltz stopped often, sometimes to store samples, but more often to consult and interact with a tablet of some sort.

Gil didn't particularly enjoy any of this. The rich stench of Jeltz's body odor was nearly overwhelming, and its hot and rough skin brushed over Gil with a distinct lack of gentility. He wondered angrily if these beings had even been endowed with a sense of touch, but he knew that wasn't right—he'd prodded Korben's eye by mistake and was hit hard enough to make him bleed. Still, he felt confident that their sense of touch had to be dulled, as if forever stuck in a thick, fleshy glove. Pain was likely a rarely-experienced sensation.

Eyes rolling as far as they could from the restricted positioning of his straps, Gil strained to lift his head and look around while Jeltz continued to prod around the orifices of his face and collect samples. Korben continued to sit at the entrance to the room, almost as if on guard. More likely, though, was that it didn't have a clue what to do in here. Gil got the impression that Korben was just the muscle in this scenario—the military man among scientists. Korben was also the only one of the four who consistently expressed disdain for Gil. He made a mental note to try and figure out why that was the case later.

The restraints on Gil's forehead were tight, so he let them smack his head back onto the exam table to rest his already-aching neck muscles. Then, rotating his head as much as he could and looking to the far right of his peripheral vision, he spotted Kif, slowly pacing the floor, eyes studying the tablet that Jeltz had held a moment ago.

But what first appeared to be independent study seemed after a few moments like Kif was actually feeding Jeltz instructions—Jeltz looked at Kif, then Gil, then Kif again, and finally at Gil's right forearm. It used one hand to turn the crook of Gil's arm upward, and produced something that resembled a syringe with the other. The syringe was empty, plunger completely depressed, and its needle seemed to be about twice as thick was Gil was familiar with.

Jeltz stared for a moment as if lost in thought, and then jammed the syringe into Gil's forearm with all the grace of a child popping a balloon with a pin. Gil screamed as sharp pain shot up his arm and raced all the way to his toes—the needle had gone straight into the bone. He felt—no, he swore he *heard*—the needle scrape against his ulna. Then Jeltz's thumb pulled back on the plunger, which intensified Gil's pain but drew nothing. It was obvious that a blood draw was being attempted, but Jeltz hadn't jabbed the needle anywhere near a vein. It didn't know what it was looking for.

Jeltz ripped the syringe out of Gil's arm and stared for a moment before jabbing it back in with the same results.

"What the hell are you doing?!" Gil screamed. Again, the syringe was tugged out and thrust back in. Out, and back in. Out, and back in. At least a dozen times, Jeltz aimlessly stabbed different areas of Gil's forearm. All the while, Gil screamed through gritted teeth. His eyes bulged from their sockets, face beet-red and tears streaming down his face. It played out like a prison stabbing.

At last, perhaps by chance alone, the needle made contact with a vein and Jeltz was able to procure a blood sample. The needle was yanked out one last time, and Gil could feel warm blood droplets forming on the surface of his cold skin. Panting, he screamed curses at Jeltz through strained vocal chords, spittle spewing from his mouth and wetting his lips. He screamed more for his own sake than Jeltz's; he knew perfectly well the thing didn't have a clue what he was saying, but he knew it could hear him, and it was cathartic to scream regardless.

Jeltz turned away and went to a nearby counter, where it began to futz with its freshly-procured samples. Gil looked down the length of his body, startled by the feeling of his shirt being pulled up to his belly button. His jeans would surely have also been pushed down a little if they hadn't already been sagging around his waist—the urine and intense sweating had made them soggy and ill fitting.

It was Roger, who once again held its strange syringe gun. It obviously wasn't meant to draw blood, because Jeltz had just done that. So what was this device's purpose? Gil's head slammed back down against the table, neck muscles exhausted from fighting against the strap wrapped over his forehead.

"What are you doing down there?" he demanded in vain. He didn't wait long to find out—using its left hand to put pressure on Gil's left side, Roger jammed the needle into the space just above Gil's left hip.

Gil wasn't a complete stranger to pain, but he'd also never felt anything quite like this. He screamed in agony, flexing every muscle in his body and once again turning red. It wasn't until much later Gil realized Roger had extracted a marrow sample from his hip bone. In light of Jeltz's performance, he had to give Roger some credit—it at least seemed to know what it was doing. It'd wielded a dangerously-large needle and hit the mark flawlessly. Still, Gil thought he'd take another dozen pricks in the arm before going through that again.

Roger finished up its procedure, withdrew the needle, and walked around the exam table to join Jeltz and Kif. En route, it stopped to ponder for a moment and then turned back around to face Gil. Approaching him again, now from the right, it reached for a button, and the left side of the exam table rose up. Gil, still tightly strapped to the table, was positioned in such a way that he could view the three aliens as they worked. *Awesome*, Gil thought. *Front row seats.*

He looked wearily at Roger and muttered, "Thanks a lot." The tone was sardonic, which was of course wasted here, but still cathartic for Gil. He continued to shiver, tears absently sliding down his face and snot dripping from his nose in thick, clear ropes. One of the whites of his eyes was now completely red—all his straining had burst a blood vessel. Roger stared for a moment, and then walked to the counter to join the other two aliens.

Gil sat for nearly an hour, suspended on the slope of the upturned table like a fly on the wall and idly staring at the backsides of Kif, Jeltz, and Roger as they all worked on their little freak show at the counter. In addition to the fluids they'd extracted from Gil, various other liquids of different colors and consistencies populated the workspace. Gil couldn't make sense of the seemingly aimless mixing, stirring, and pouring, but could tell they worked with a purpose. It seemed to go on forever.

But at last, they turned around. Kif now held a syringe gun in his hand similar to the one Roger had used to extract Gil's marrow, but this one was already full. A translucent grey sludge sloshed around the glass tube, at which Gil took just one look before raging against his steep table.

He was fearful Kif had a plan to shoot it back into him. And next thing you knew, poor Gil would be exploding all over the walls, only to be mopped up and burned to ashes in their oven so these things could go pick up some other unfortunate soul. They would shrug and think to each other, "Well, you can't make an omelet without breaking a few eggs! Back to the drawing board!"

This wasn't the case, however; as Korben got up to join them, Kif raised the syringe and planted it into its own rib cage. Kif winced a little. It was the first time, Gil later realized, any of them had shown any signs of pain. He stared in stunned silence, and the aliens all stared in much the same manner.

For a long time—nearly another hour—nothing happened. Every eye in the room stared at the tiny hole in Kif's chest made by the syringe. Eventually, the four aliens intensified their gaze and brought their heads closer to the dot—they had noticed a change. At first, Gil couldn't make anything out, but after a few more moments, he too saw the focus of their scrutiny: the area around the needle's insertion point was turning grey.

Initially just a small cloud, the grey color slowly swirled outward like a miniature galaxy over Kif's skin. From its chest, down to its stomach, then its legs, and finally terminating at its toes, the new color seemed to be engulfing Kif's entire body. Their shoulders sank and their heads lowered—it looked like relief. Roger and Jeltz reached for each other's hands, and soon, all four of them embraced each other in a circle. Gil, brow furrowed, stared in confusion.

After a long pause, Korben approached Gil, lowered the table back down to a level position, and released his restraints.

Gil sat up and let his legs hang off the edge of the table as Korben, Jeltz, Kif, and Roger exited back to the corridor. But as Kif crossed the threshold and turned around to close the room, it noticed that Gil hadn't gotten to his feet yet. The rich grey tone emanating from the dot on its chest continued to grow and cover Kif like paint on a canvas. At this point, it looked like a grey toga draped over Kif's pale body.

It gestured to him, encouraging him to follow along, but Gil wasn't quite ready to move yet—he couldn't wrap his mind around what had just happened. He had been their lab rat, for what purpose he didn't know, but they seemed to have accomplished something. And with their purpose now complete, their interest in Gil had vanished. Perhaps this meant they'd take him home?

Gil put his feet on the floor and started towards Kif, who seemed to be wearing a turtleneck. The grey tone had covered its appendages and now slowly crept up its neck.

With mere feet between them, Kif's left eye started to twitch. Gil stopped in his tracks. Kif's legs give way like rubber as it fell to its knees, and then smacked face-first onto the ground. Eyes closed, its entire body now twitched. Korben, Roger, and Jeltz all whirled around and rushed to Kif's aid, whose new grey tone at last crept into its bulbous head.

Roger turned Kif over on its back and elevated its head. Kif, no longer simply shaking, convulsed brutally in Roger's lap. Kif's eyes fluttered. A foamy, yellow, foul-smelling liquid bubbled over and spilled out of its mouth. Once again, Gil was treated to the unsettling sound of its vocal chords, undulating like a viciously strangled animal.

Korben rose up from its haunches and bolted down the corridor at a speed Gil wouldn't have thought possible, and another of the cog's teeth opened to reveal a room Gil could only see a sliver of. It was far enough away that the curve of the corridor mostly obscured it.

A moment later, Korben was bounding back towards the examination room with a device in its hand similar in shape to a large thumb tack—large enough that Korben's hand wrapped around the base like the hilt of a sword. The hilt had a brushed-nickel finish, and a single button at its base. The business end of it, a large, jet-black spike, was roughly four inches long.

Korben leaped into the air with its right arm outstretched like a baseball player touching the home plate. As the giant came down, the tip of the device crashed cleanly into Kif's forehead all the way up to the hilt. Holding it steady, Korben used its thumb to depress the device's single button.

The device illuminated red and blared like a foghorn for a moment. Gil winced and covered his ears. When it stopped, the area was once again filled with the gargling, choked undulation of Kif's voice as it convulsed in Roger's lap.

Korben held one hand firmly around the device, the other pressed firmly against Kif's chin to hold the head stable. After another short moment, Kif inhaled for the last time. Its eyes now open wide, body stiff as a board, Kif let out a muffled, bone-chilling shriek that went on for the better part of half a minute. When its lungs had completely emptied out, its body went limp. The device illuminated green for a moment and emitted a short, pleasant, high-pitched warble. Korben withdrew it, leaving behind an execution-style bullet hole in the corpse's cranium—Kif was dead.

Gil stood frozen in the exam room and simply gaped, baffled by what had happened. They had taken a sample of his blood—a proper sample this time, through sheer persistence—had mixed it with his bone marrow and God-knows-what else, and injected it back into one of their own. Gil had no idea why. He only knew the obvious: things hadn't gone as the aliens had hoped.

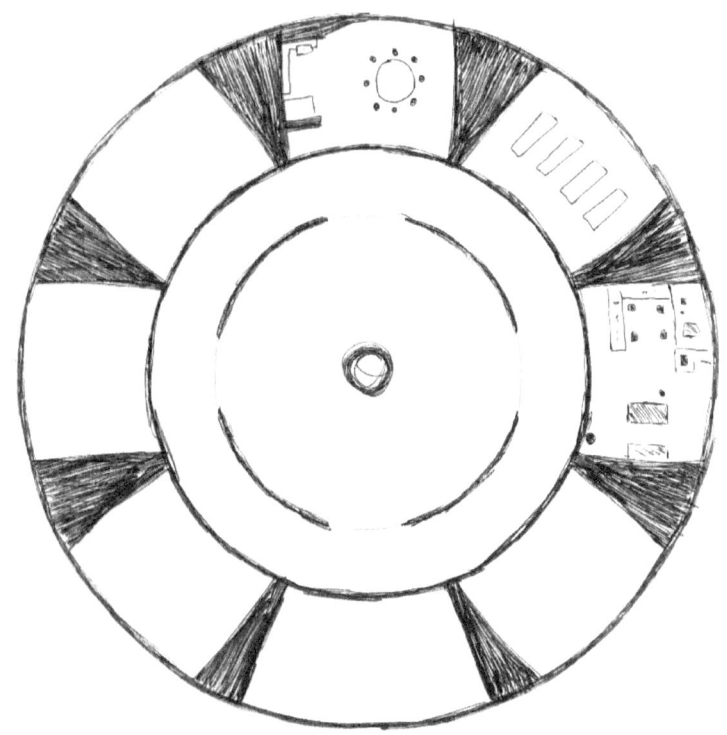

Chapter Five: Dearly Departed

Three beings stood around their fallen companion and, for a moment, they had completely forgotten about Gil.

Standing there in his soiled clothes, having still not moved an inch since Kif's face slapped the metal floor, Gil tried to make sense of the situation. *Like chickens*, he thought.

As a child, Gil had once gone to a local farm with his parents to bring home a pumpkin for Halloween. In addition to the festive pumpkins, there were also various common farm animals for visitors to interact with. Gil had ridden a pony, stopped to pet the sheep, and giggled at the filthy pigs rolling around in the mud.

When he approached the chicken coop, a young boy was being pulled out of it by his angry mother. He had entered the coop to have a bit of fun getting the chickens all worked up, but accidentally stepped on one of the birds. After a loud shriek, it just lay there on its side, lifting up its head to look around.

Blissfully unaware, little Gil wrapped his tiny fingers around the chicken wire and peered inside the coop just as all the other chickens descended upon their injured cellmate and viciously pecked it to death. This disturbing scene sent the five-year-old into hysterics, and his parents took him straight home—no pumpkin that year.

Much later in life, Gil learned that this was a fairly normal occurrence. If a chicken became injured, the others might turn on the bird and peck it to death. Similarly, there didn't seem to be any attempt made to bring Kif back from his sudden seizure. Nearly as soon as it had begun, the only apparent option was to jam a spike through its skull and put it out of its misery.

Gil had to admit to himself, of course, that he didn't have a clue what conversation may have transpired between them. For all he knew, Kif may have begged for Korben to drive that spike through its skull. It was just as likely they'd given up out of sheer lack of medical knowledge as it was that their logical minds mentally exhausted every course of action and knew it would end in failure.

He snapped out of his daze—Roger had lifted Kif's corpse up into its arms, and the three of them moved into the corridor. Gil followed, still seemingly unnoticed, and the walls of the exam room silently slid shut once they had all stepped out of the area.

The beings glanced at the wall containing the center room. Jeltz lifted his right hand and interacted with a sequence of lights on the wall to once again open a door into the large round room. Once the clear pane was out of the way, Roger walked just past the threshold and dropped Kif's body onto the ground. The small corpse hit the floor like a sack of fertilizer.

With Roger back in the corridor and the window pane closed, the three of them stared in silent eulogy at the undignified heap that was Kif. On cue, Gil thought, *he was the only one of you who hadn't made me bleed.* He had a feeling that height played a role in whatever their equivalent of testosterone levels were, and was genuinely a little sad to see the most docile of them be the one to croak. *Why couldn't that big idiot, Korben, have been the test candidate?*

And then a darker, more selfish thought entered Gil's head, and he wondered if this corpse was going to be his new roommate.

Now Korben lifted a hand to the wall and fiddled with some sort of display that had materialized under his touch. Gil glanced over and saw the strange device in the alien's free hand that had been driven into Kif's skull—it was filthy, covered in all manner of yellowed vomit and guts. He looked back through the window and saw that the spinning orange disc in the middle of the room started to rise up. It maintained a silent, constant ascent until stopping mere inches below the silvery protrusions from the ceiling. It had to be about eight feet off the ground. Gil could see his puddle of urine pooled in the dip of the room's center.

The giant continued to press phantom buttons and slide its finger along the display until a wide-circle outline in the floor of the center room began to recede.

At first level with the ground, Gil watched as a one-inch wall formed around the perimeter of his urine. Then two inches. And then three. After several more inches, perhaps eight altogether, its descent revealed screaming blackness. The yellow puddle disappeared in a flash of vapor. Kif's body turned over and slid raggedly towards the opening—first slowly, and then at a literal breakneck pace.

The corpse flew along the floor and smacked into the metal panels surrounding the opening. Its belly wedged itself into the opening and went first into the blackness like a fist squeezing a ripe tomato. Kif bent over backwards, snapping like a bundle of kindling as it threaded through the opening; skull dashing against the edge of the void and exploding like a hardboiled egg from a slingshot.

Bits of grey matter flew upwards before quickly changing course and reversing through the opening. Shortly afterwards, Gil's day-old mess of congealed vomit was also sucked into the void, leaving only smears behind; the vacuum had claimed everything.

Eventually, the room grew silent. Only a few pieces of visible matter remained, floating freely and lazily bumping into the walls. After Korben made a few more gestures on the wall, the opening closed, the orange disc lowered, and what looked like the jets of fire extinguishers erupted all along the ceiling.

The glass pane slid open yet again, and it was as if nothing had ever happened. Korben slowly turned around, and then started at the sight of Gil—it had completely forgotten about him. It grabbed him by the shoulder and pushed him into the cog's center room. Gil whirled around and started back towards the three of them.

"No, please!" Gil cried. "Please don't make me stay in—let me sleep in the corridor! What's the harm anyway?! I can't even open the— "

Korben took its right hand and made contact with Gil's ribcage, pushing him back with enough force to sweep him off his feet. As the doors to the center room began to slide shut, he flew backwards, hitting the back of his head against the hard floor and skidding to a stop just outside the center of the room.

Gil was knocked unconscious. And this time, he did dream. He was in a hospital. Wearing a paper robe and lying in a dirty bed, cruel doctors dug into him with bare hands. Their red eyes were gigantic, the irises a mess of piano wires tugging at the bottomless pits of their pupils. And when they pulled off their green surgical masks, horribly oversized and maniacal grins bore impossibly-long, yellow teeth embedded in blackened gums.

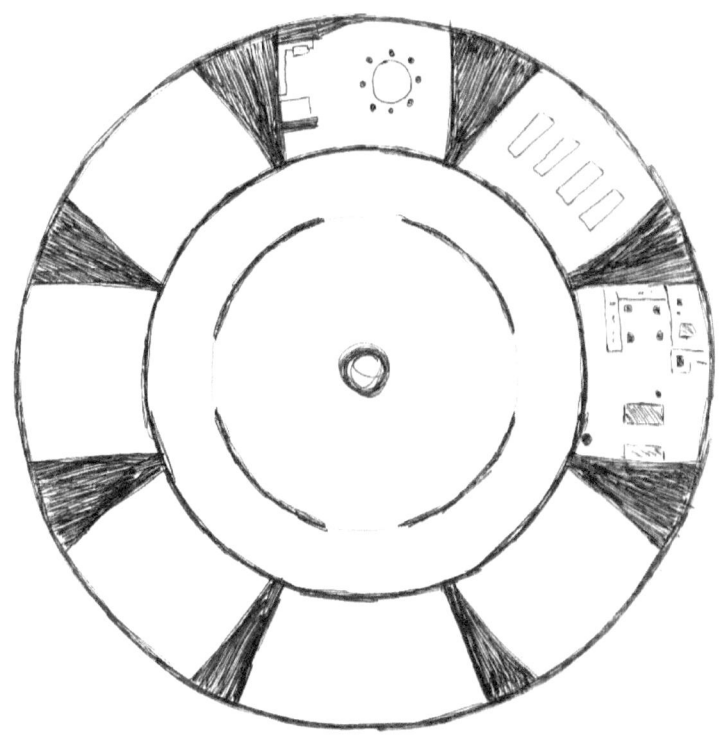

CHAPTER SIX: CULTURE SHOCK

A dull pain forced Gil from his dreams, and he was grateful for it. He must have been trying to roll over in his sleep again, but the soreness in his left hip made that a difficult proposition. He felt his lower back with this hand. *Pretty tender*, he thought.

His head was pointing to the orange disc like an arrow—before the attempted roll that woke him, he'd been in the exact position Korben had put him in and he didn't have a clue how long he'd been out. The disc's glow once again reached through the large area like a campfire, which meant that the lights were still off. His entire body was freezing save for his head which, due to its close proximity to the spinning disc, burned as if it were in an oven.

He shimmied himself into a position so that he faced the disc again. The dried blood on his right arm flaked and fluttered to the floor in crimson snowflakes. Pulling his knees to his chest and placing his hands close to the disc to warm them up, he stared uneasily at the space below. In addition to all the other dangers lurking here, enough to fuel a lifetime of nightmares, Gil was also just a few touchpad gestures away from being sucked down the drain like dirty bathwater. It was a new horror, unlike anything he'd ever seen, and he couldn't imagine a more gruesome way to go.

Gil's body steadily warmed, but his shivering continued. Still waking up, he also became gradually aware of a dull headache and a mild discomfort in his gut. It felt like the stomach cramps of diarrhea, likely from the raw beef he'd consumed—and he was already half-dehydrated from the outset. *Good*, he thought. *I'll just shit myself to death, and they can come in here and sift through the muck with a fine tooth comb to get what they're after.*

His own sarcasm somehow flying over his head, Gil sat bolt upright. That sounded terrible—he didn't want that at all. Not here, wherever the hell this was, and he certainly didn't like the thought of his own corpse being strained into a fine paste and sucked through a slot after he'd croaked. *Maybe I can find out where the hell I am and figure out a way to get outta here.* He worked his way to his feet, disbelieving he'd ever complained about soreness before now, and then with wide eyes promptly dropped his jeans and squatted. He was so thankful, despite everything else, that liquid pooled to the center.

When he'd finished, he started towards the edge of the room.

Using his growing collection of bodily fluid smears as a roadmap, Gil located the first door he'd seen when introductions were made. He lifted his hand and touched the wall next to the panel, but nothing happened. He tried again, but still, no luck.

How the hell is this thing supposed to work? he asked himself. However the interface worked, he knew it couldn't rely on resistive technology because there was no screen to resist his touch—he'd seen the aliens touch pretty much anywhere near the edge of the moving panels, and a phantom display would simply appear at the point of contact. It was exactly like a context menu on his laptop; no matter where his cursor was on the screen, a right click of the mouse would make a tiny menu appear adjacent to it. Similarly, the interface appeared high up when Korben used it, but much closer to the floor for the shorter aliens.

He knew it also couldn't be capacitive technology, because he was as good a conductor of electricity as they were. *Perhaps it's heat sensitive?* Gil recalled the immense heat the aliens gave off and wondered if their systems relied on temperature, but simply weren't calibrated to detect something as comparatively cold as his human finger. He concluded this to be the case after a contemplative moment, but he had an idea.

Balling his right hand into a fist, he rubbed it furiously against the wall. His hand burned from the friction after only a few seconds, but there was still no response. It wasn't long before he began to doubt himself. *This was a dumb idea*, he thought. *They wouldn't even be able to turn on the heat without setting off every display in here. No way they're heat-sensitive.* But just as he was about to give up, with fresh tears welling up in his eyes, a display slowly flickered into view and hung just off the surface of the wall. Two icons appeared and, desperately scared of losing the heat he'd built up, Gil quickly touched one at random.

A panel and window parted ways, creating a wide exit into the corridor.

"I am a *genius*," he declared in a whisper. He started towards the exit, then suddenly froze in his tracks. Suppose one of the aliens heard the door open and came running over? *God, suppose Korben's on his way?*

Gil had hoped the lights being dimmed would indicate the aliens had sought sleep, but he of course had no idea if this was the case. For all he knew, they might throw Gil into the center room at any arbitrary time, shut the lights off, and then continue to work on their science project with their lab rat safely tucked away.

He stood expectantly for a moment, waiting for something to reach out and grab him, but nothing happened. And after a few minutes of uninterrupted silence, he finally gathered up his courage and sallied forth.

He looked through the porthole directly in front of him and saw only darkness; however, the various instruments along this room's planked wall assured Gil that this particular tooth of the cog had to be important. He told himself he'd come back to it, but first, he had to make sure that the aliens weren't stirring. He remembered passing a porthole that looked to have something like beds inside, immediately to the right of the kitchen. And he knew that room was on the opposite end of where he stood now, so he made a half circle around the corridor.

The kitchen was dimly lit, but he could still make out its details. Consulting his mental map, he continued on and then slowly crept up to the next porthole. A dim blue light spilled out, and inside, Gil was relieved to see the pale white bodies of Jeltz, Roger, and Korben sleeping peacefully in their hard, coverless beds. The bed between Jeltz and Roger was, of course, empty. Gil shook his head. *What the hell were you guys even trying to do?* He turned around and headed back through the corridor.

After another furious moment of rubbing, Gil managed to activate and spread open the planks to the kitchen. Its lights flickered on. He shuffled around, looking for something with a spout, and was thankful to spy a turn valve next to a set of the same, odd drinking glasses he's seen earlier. *Thank God*, he thought. He'd never been as thirsty as he was now. He turned the valve, filled up one of the glasses, and drank. He repeated this several times, until he felt the water slosh around in his belly like a bota bag.

He constantly looked over his shoulder, unable to shake the nervous feeling that he was being watched. And yet, a growing part of him didn't care—if they were going to treat him like a lab rat, he'd sneak around like a rat. And if they caught him, they'd throw him back into his prison cell.

Continuing to search, Gil found something of a refrigerator and retrieved a thin cut of the same raw meat he'd consumed before. He didn't necessarily want to exacerbate what he was now sure was clearly diarrhea, but he also didn't want to go hungry. He grabbed a plate and decided to get out of the kitchen.

Walking past the threshold and back into the corridor, Gil triggered the room's planks to slide back into place and seal the kitchen. After stopping off at the center room again to take care of more business—thank god that door remained open—he walked back to the kitchen porthole, plate in hand, and continued where he left off. Turning back around, he moved to the left and peered in though the next porthole, where he saw what looked like a sink and a series of showers. Out loud this time, Gil whispered, "Thank God."

His right hand now terribly tender, Gil rubbed the panel with his left and made his way through the unfolding planks of the corridor. He walked straight to the sink, set down his plate of raw meat, and looked for a faucet. He found none, but knew that it had to be a sink—there was a drain at the bottom of the basin.

As he reached to the bottom of the basin to feel for moisture, a thin, horizontal line at the midpoint of the sink shot out a steaming sheet of hot water. Gil withdrew his hand with a start, but still found himself burned by the water's scalding heat. He sucked through his teeth and vigorously shook his right hand from the elbow.

A quick scan of the showers revealed the same thin strips overhead. *Sheesh*, he thought, *they wash in this?* He walked over to one of the showers and swiped his hand through the air. Sure enough, a steaming jet of scalding hot water fell like a pane of glass to the shower floor. *No shower for me.*

Gil walked back to the sink. He couldn't clean himself up in the shower, but he had another idea. First, he gingerly touched the surface area at the back of the basin—it was raised higher than the rest of the sink and just above the motion sensor. It burned, and he drew his hand back; but instead of wincing this time, he muttered, "Eureka."

Peeling the cut of meat from the plate, Gil slapped it onto the raised portion of the sink and was delighted to see it quietly sizzle. Now, he was going to wash up.

With his next meal cooking, Gil slipped his shirt off and twirled it around in the sink like a cat toy. Predictably, the water jets sprang to life and battered his shirt until it was soaking wet and steaming. He set it on the adjacent counter in a heap, kicked off his sneakers, and pulled his socks off.

Delicately, he dangled his socks over the jets and soaked them as well before setting them on the counter. He repeated this process with his jeans, and finally, his soiled boxer shorts.

Now naked, he looked himself over. His body was filthy and covered in red splotches. He wondered for a moment if the rashes were caused by the disc in the center room, but thought better of it—more likely, it was just too much time soaking in his own sweat, piss, and stomach acid.

He groped his soaking shirt. Still hot, but now manageable, he picked it up and wrung it out over his head. Water trickled down the length of his body and splashed onto the floor, and he used the remaining moisture in the cloth to scrub himself down from head to toe. He wasn't going to get anywhere near clean with this sponge bath, but for the time being, simply not being sticky would suffice just fine.

Careful to avoid the hot water, he dangled and sprayed his shirt again before setting it aside. It was time to wring out and get his clothes back on now, but first, he had to tend to his meal—he used his thumb and index finger to pinch a corner of the fillet, pick it up, and flip it over. It didn't look particularly appetizing, but it was definitely cooking.

Gil wrung out his socks, boxers, and jeans as much as he could, and then put them on. They were, of course, still wet, but he didn't mind. Unlike the cold temperature of the center room, the corridor and connecting chambers felt like a hot summer night. It would be nice to walk around in something cool for a little while.

He put his shirt back on and, while the cut of mystery meat finished cooking, he looked around a bit. Conspicuously, there was nothing resembling a toilet. He'd been wondering about that from the get-go— they didn't seem to have anything going on down below. But they had to create waste, didn't they? How did they reproduce? Were there even multiple sexes?

And most baffling of all, why the hell were they naked? Were they honestly so advanced that they'd evolved beyond a need for clothes? Gil scoffed at that. *What does that even mean?* Wherever they were from, did they not need protection against the elements? Perhaps they simply found clothes uncomfortable. Certainly it was a concept they'd understood; they seemed to easily work around Gil's clothes during both of his exams.

There was one device between the sink and showers Gil couldn't make heads or tails of. It was a strange cross between a garbage can, a bird's wings, and one of those old-fashioned scales found in a doctor's office.

It seemed obvious that one was meant to stand at the base of the device. A long pole rose up from one end of it, leading to two large, symmetrical metal wings covered in dozens of dull prongs—almost like a hair brush. He stared sideways at the device for a moment with a raised eyebrow, and then had an epiphany.

"The mud on their backs..." He trailed off, and then tittered. "They crap outta their backs." He laughed again, finally understanding that the strange device he saw was something of a toilet.

Gil peeled the fillet off the back of the sink and slapped it onto his plate. He'd already been drenched in a fresh coat of sweat, but it felt great in the still heat. Somewhat clean and with a meal in hand, he headed for the room he promised himself he'd return to.

He passed the beds on his way, and cautiously peered through the porthole again. They hadn't moved. With his newfound freedom, he briefly mulled over the logistics of tricking one or more of them into the center room and subjecting them to the same fate as their former crewmember. But he shook it off. Gil was the only guest aboard this cruise ship who had to give a hand job to every door he came across; the others could simply open whatever door he closed and send him straight to hell with a single blow. So he supposed sneaking around like a rat wasn't so bad, and he moved on.

The next room he reached was the exam room, which he passed at full speed. And the room to the right of the exam room had an additional row of four beds. Gil was initially outraged by this, seeing that they had extra room yet still kept him locked in a dank toilet; however, he quickly realized he'd have liked it even less in there. The beds, now that he got a good look at them, seemed nightmarish. The mattress seemed from the porthole to be soft rubber, with a dip where his upper back would be. They were also narrower than a twin mattress. So he decided he was better off, and continued. He finally found himself face to face again with the very first porthole he'd seen. Both of his hands were rubbed raw at this point, but Gil Sanders was on a roll and he had another idea. With a grin, he picked up the cooked meat in his right hand and pressed it to the space under the porthole.

Gil quickly brought the bottom of his shirt over his right hand and wiped the greasy meat juice from the panels as they gave way. He was pleased with himself—that had indeed been a good idea.

The lights flickered on, and he was greeted with five tall-backed chairs behind a large bay of controls that ran the entire width of the 20-foot room. The chair in the center had a taller back than the other four, and the control space in front of it included a strange-looking flight stick. Above the control bay, the tapered ceiling consisted of the same planks that closed off each room from the central corridor. Just as with all the other rooms, everything here seemed to be constructed of the same dark silver. With equal parts curiosity and anxiety, Gil saw this was a cockpit.

He took a seat at the tall chair, its padding reminded him of a mouse pad's gel wrist guard, and looked over the deep control deck. The controls were thankfully tactile, unlike the phantom touch-screen controls in the corridor and center room, but most of them were still unrecognizable to Gil. The only pieces of machinery that Gil could make any sense of were the aforementioned flight stick, and a sliding knob with what looked like an illustration of a car windshield above it.

He tentatively placed his hand on the slider before pushing it to the right. Silently, the planks above the control board parted in the middle and slid to the left and right, revealing a gigantic window that spanned the width of the room.

Gil's mouth, full of chewed meat, hung open. In front of him, in sharper detail than any picture or video could have ever shown, he watched as the craters Pavlov, Tsiolkovski, Fermi, Milne, and Hilbert came into view. He didn't actually know any of these landmarks, and in fact, stared for a long time wondering what seemed so unfamiliar about the landscape out the window. He knew it was The Moon, but it didn't look right—it didn't match the picture in his mind from the thousands of times he'd seen it in the night sky. At last, it occurred to him that it was The Moon's far side. And it was beautiful.

Hold up, he thought, *I'm in space.* The possibility that he'd left Earth had been a dormant fear of his for a while now. It had been a good possibility from the start, and he supposed it was blatantly obvious after Kif's exit, but this was the first time he'd had visual confirmation: he sat aboard a spacefaring cliché, also known as a flying saucer, floating behind The Moon.

Gil resumed eating, but didn't take his eyes off the window. Not yet. He absently touched the stubble on his face with his free hand. The past few days—or rather, the past few indiscernible periods of time—had been some of the worst in his entire life. Never mind his captors' unsettling appearance; he'd been kidnapped, brutalized, stabbed, and imprisoned, all in the interest of a goal that they either couldn't communicate to him or just didn't care to. But as he stared out into space, he couldn't help but feel strangely sentimental. So few humans had ever ventured beyond earth's atmosphere, and fewer still had ever had the opportunity to see what he was seeing now. He felt oddly thankful.

Continuing to munch on his fillet, Gil's mind gradually turned back to his captors.

He recalled reading an online article—in general, Gil had a lot of time to browse the web—where the author posited that alien abduction claims were nothing more than deeply repressed memories of alleged victims' birth experiences. And Gil liked that; it was a nice and neat explanation that made *sense* to him.

The alleged abductees would usually claim to be taken from a comfortable place by a bright light. Then, people with huge white heads and black eyes would stand around them and do completely unrecallable and benign things. No one could ever remember; they only knew that they had been on a table, where they were poked and prodded in such a way that no evidence of the encounter would exist. More often than not, people would shrug and simply respond that they ran "tests." Tests like a nurse would conduct on a newborn under a bright light.

It was convenient enough that the trend of abduction claims seemed to coincide with the cultural shift of births occurring at a hospital instead of at home, but what had really driven it home for Gil was that he knew there were limitations to what newborns could actually see. Their underdeveloped eyes couldn't see much from far away, and only starkly contrasting colors—like black and white—really popped out. In fact, he'd heard that women's nipples would apparently darken during pregnancy to increase the contrast and make them more noticeable to newborns. With that in mind, he could easily see why a face in a surgical mask with dark eyes could be blurred into the visage of something that appeared alien.

Gil smiled and shook his head, thinking, *I really did like that explanation.* But his experiences thus far had too much in common with all those stories. He hadn't seen any bright lights, but—he'd forgotten about this until now—he was literally plucked from his front yard and sucked into the air. And now, here he was on a space ship, parked behind The Moon, and held captive by mysterious creatures whose likeness was so ubiquitous that popular culture had come to refer to them simply as "Greys."

With this in mind, Gil had to operate under the assumption that all of the outlandish stories he'd heard—even the *weird* ones—might actually be true. This meant, of course, that as a species, they didn't necessarily all have the same motivations for visiting.

He tried to recall all the abduction tales he could, and found at least some difficulty separating actual claims from deliberately fictional TV shows. He wished he had his smartphone with him, knowing such information would be just an internet search away.

There was that logger in Arizona... they made a movie about that. He got picked up and found himself on an exam table surrounded by a few beings likely not too dissimilar in description from Gil's hosts. He claimed to have been so startled by the encounter that he leaped from the table and then brandished a long and clear pole he found nearby. He apparently acted so macho, swinging around that clear stick, that *they* ran away from *him.* He began to wander around the ship and was finally coaxed into cooperating by some other beings who looked more human than the others—hair, lips, and a dull smile. They led him to the exam table, he lay back down, and then things went dark. When he came to, he was near a gas station, filthy and sore.

There was a farmer from Brazil who claimed to have been picked up by some beings who had been observing him for weeks. After finally making contact with him and inviting him aboard their ship, they stuck him in a room with a naked woman who flatly instructed him to have sex with her. And that was it—when it was over, they gave him the boot and flew away.

There was that couple from New Hampshire who'd allegedly been abducted while driving home and given mostly harmless physicals. *That had to be something like 80 years ago, at this point.*

There were also countless accounts on primetime TV Gil saw when he was a kid, ranging from intergalactic sightseeing, to cloning, stealing pregnancies, *planting* pregnancies, all the way up to the ultimate alien cliché: anal probing. Gil rolled his eyes when that crossed his mind.

He shook his head again, but this time in frustration. *That's just stupid. I refuse to believe that all these ridiculous stories are true. Some of them, maybe, but a trip here just to be... voyeurs?* Gil snorted. *Hell, I'd even buy that they were trying to cross-breed, but if any of that wasn't nonsense, why is this outing straying so far from the norm?*

No, they'd have to be separate, unmonitored trips. They must have opened the cruise lines up to anyone, allowing scientists and perverts alike to visit at will. But what of safety? Countries on Earth who met for the first time would unwittingly infect each other with foreign diseases, killing thousands in the process, and these things don't even wear clothes. Despite their tech, the Greys were so reckless as to—

Gil choked on his food, the word, "Greys" suddenly hanging in his mind like a fishhook. *Grey?* he thought. *These things aren't grey.* It was one of the first things he noticed when he met them. After a few coughs and a firm hand to the chest, he redirected his bite of food and, while panting, mentally ran through a couple of recent events. He recalled the flicker of grey he'd seen in Jeltz's finger when it absorbed his blood. Then, of course, there was Kif who, in its arrogance, injected itself with some of Gil's fluids and briefly turned grey before dying. Otherwise, they were completely white, almost sickly—like the pale white and homesick protagonist from the latter half of *E.T.*

That was exactly like Jeltz earlier, when he passed out in the kitchen, Gil thought.

And then suddenly, it hit him: "They're sick," he whispered.

Gil laughed out loud—he couldn't help it. It was all just so ironic! *For all their technological advancements, for all the decades of visits to Earth to study us...* In their extreme, literally naked carelessness, what if one of them ended up catching a virus and bringing it back home? *Dysentery on an intergalactic scale, perhaps.*

It all made so much sense now. His captors didn't seem to know what they were doing, having no idea how to communicate with Gil, much less draw blood from him—but what if these idiots were the only Greys left not bedridden... or dead? *So here they are now, blindly taking shots in the dark in the hopes that they can find a cure.* Gil lightly touched his perforated forearm. *And they're not exactly doing a bang-up job.*

He also recalled that his friendly neighbor could have just as likely been the subject, but the aliens couldn't pull it off at first. *Hell, they were so inexperienced with whatever technology they were using that they'd almost abducted a sedan.*

There were still a few things that didn't seem to make sense. Gil didn't understand what they could possibly be infected with, especially since the cure for whatever it was seemed to exist somewhere within his perfectly unremarkable human body. Maybe it was something he'd been vaccinated with? Maybe it was just a common human infection and they had to harvest white blood cells?

Then, of course, there was the question of where they came from. Even with Gil's limited knowledge of—or interest in—Earth's neighboring planets, it was obvious to Gil that they didn't live anywhere within the solar system. These things breathed air, which, far as he knew, was only available on Earth. That put Mars out of the question, and everything past Mars was either nothing but gas or nothing but ice. *Or something like that,* he thought.

Okay, he continued, *so that puts them somewhere in a galaxy far, far away*. But how did they get here? Or, a better question, how had they made so many repeat trips in a matter of decades? He'd read recently about a satellite, launched years ago, that had finally left the solar system and gone into deep space. He knew from the Apollo missions that even a trip to The Moon took four days. The only thing he knew of that could travel at light speed—aside from light—were radio waves. So had they discovered a faster method of traveling? Or perhaps it was something Gil couldn't conceive.

More harrowing, though, was how they all treated Gil—especially Korben, who seemed to have a personal vendetta against him. Had it made up its mind Gil was personally responsible for their ailment? Had they perceived the infection as an attack? Perhaps its size simply made it more aggressive, but if so, why bother bringing it along? Gil didn't know.

He'd finished his meal. Gil's stomach felt a little better, but he knew he'd have to use the facilities of his holding cell at least a few more times. He stood up and took one last look at the view outside. But as he reached for the knob to close the window, he caught a whiff of an unpleasant odor.

Gil whirled around, greeted briefly by twin reflections of his own startled face. It was Korben, or more specifically, those gigantic eyes, staring at Gil with palpable rage.

He shouted in surprise, falling backwards and landing on the control bay with his back mashing against an untold number of buttons and switches. *Oh God*, his mind screamed, *they woke up!*

Korben lifted both its arms to grab Gil, who instinctively held up the greasy plate to shield his face. Korben froze for only an instant as it put the pieces together: its now-clean prisoner had sneaked into several of the ship's rooms while they slept.

Dumbfounded and furious, it sent its balled-up right fist towards the plate, smashing right through it like Styrofoam and making contact with Gil's face. The pain was terrible; the shattered not-quite-glass material of the plate cut into Gil's face and exploded into the air in a dozen different directions. Bits of it dug into the knuckles of Korben's right hand, sticking out like peppermint bark.

Gil was dazed—he screamed in pain, but heard only a faint ringing sound. His head now resting against the surface of the control board, only a swirl of dark silver with a hint of white filled his vision.

The hint of white, as it turned out, was Korben's gigantic hands, reaching for and wrapping themselves around Gil's throat. Underneath the flexible and slightly cushioned skin of the alien's hands were what felt like ten metal bars. And as he was lifted into the air, the burden of Gil's bodyweight once again hung from his neck.

Two spinning visions of Korben's screaming face slowly converged into one. Despite the screaming, Gil heard nothing but a faint, high-pitched hum in his ears. Unable to breath, he stared flatly at his own reflection in Korben's eyes with his hands hanging on the creature's wrists in a vain attempt to support himself. Korben, intentionally or not, was choking the life out of him. He began to see spots— shimmering specks of white danced in his field of vision.

With sound finally coming back into his ears, he heard something unfamiliar. *Like pixie dust*, he thought, whatever that meant. And then, a gradual but startling feeling of weightlessness rose in him. He opened his eyes and, forcing them to focus one last time, discovered the specks of white were actually pieces of the shattered plate—they were floating. The sound he'd heard was the little bits bouncing off the walls.

Korben must have noticed at the same time, because its grip around Gil loosened, who then inhaled with all the force of windstorm. And when its hands were completely removed from his neck, Gil remained airborne. The artificial gravity in the ship was gone; Gil had flipped a switch or pressed a button when his back hit the control board, and now everything not nailed down moved freely. Korben, for the first time, looked scared. Who knew what was now floating free within the eight chambers of the ship?

Gil, gasping for air, needed to get away from Korben—it was the only thought in his head. Gil floundered for a moment, then lifted his legs and thrust both feet into Korben's chest. They both flew back from each other.

In a panic, his trembling hands shot up above his head with just enough time to press them against the window and avoid bashing his head. He hit hard, surprised at how much force the kick had produced. He turned around to face the glass, seeing the moon again and fogging the view with his heavy breath.

He was stunned for a moment, in fresh awe of the lunar landscape out the window, but shook himself—he had to move. Scrambling and reaching for purchase wherever he could, Gil situated himself so that his feet pressed against the glass. He looked out of the room, which felt like looking straight up from the bottom of a long stairwell. And at the top, Roger and Jeltz hovered in the doorway leading to the kitchen chamber.

To his right, he saw Korben; it had kicked off the wall to the center room and was now careening towards Gil with amazing speed. With only a second to act, but without a plan, Gil pushed his hands against the control board to bend at the knees, and then blindly kicked off.

Gil screamed in surprise as he flew out of the cockpit, across the width of the corridor, and into the center room. He furiously waved his arms around in an attempt to slow down, but there was no effect—without any resistance working against him, he raced along at the same pace as when he'd launched himself.

Passing in front of the spinning disc with the stalactites from the ceiling brushing against his back, something gripped his ankle and yanked. It was Korben. It had kicked off the far end of the cockpit just like Gil—but with much more force than he'd been able to muster—and caught up to him in seconds. It spun Gil around and gathered up a wad of the front of Gil's shirt in its left fist. Behind him, the glass pane was sliding shut; Roger and Jeltz had initiated the closing sequence to contain Gil in his prison cell.

He flew past the threshold and into the opposite end of the corridor, where his back thumped against the planked wall leading to the kitchen. It knocked the wind out of him. Korben roared at him from the center room, but to Gil's relief, the giant was behind the sliding glass—it didn't clear the door in time.

But something wasn't right; Korben also still held Gil's shirt in its balled-up fist. Perplexed, Gil took a closer look at Korben and saw its left arm was... gone. Korben hadn't been roaring in anger, but pain. Just below the shoulder, all that remained was what looked like a putrefied beef wellington—impossibly thick skin surrounding a disgusting mass of oozing, grey-green raw meat with a single thin circle of bone in the center. Like a thick weed tugged apart, the wound was wet with milky green syrup, but didn't drip—it just oozed.

Gil, though fascinated by this strange anatomy, didn't have time to dwell. He looked to his left and saw Roger and Jeltz pin-balling down the corridor. Ahead, a seething Korben fiddled with something to the left of the window. The window started to open. Gil ripped the severed arm off his shirt, threw it, and launched himself to the right.

Bounding off the walls in a zigzag pattern—a technique he'd just observed in the other two aliens—Gil made his way through the corridor. His obvious folly was that he'd eventually come around the bend and run into the other two aliens, but he was hysterical—he wasn't thinking rationally. Every ounce of his mental processing was devoted to putting distance between himself and the huge alien. He was already panting, breath burning like fire in his throat, but in that moment he'd loop around the ship's circular corridor until his heart gave out if it meant never having to face the tall one.

As he came around the bend to the section of wall containing the cockpit, Gil saw both Roger and Jeltz tinkering at the control bay. Gil gradually started to glide downwards until he brushed against the floor and stopped entirely. He tried desperately to pick himself up and run, but his body refused—he was exhausted.

Panting and defeated, Gil rolled onto his back and looked behind himself. Korben walked towards him with purpose, dragging its severed left arm along the floor of the corridor. The alien looked rabid. Gil shielded his face with his hands.

"I'm sorry!" he cried. "It was an accident! I didn't mean for your—"

But predictably, Korben was not listening. When it approached Gil, it swung its severed arm into the air and beat him with it until he lay unconscious. Eventually, Roger and Jeltz would intervene, wrapping themselves around Korben to stop it and hold it down; they weren't yet finished with Gil. The intervention was likely the only reason he survived that encounter.

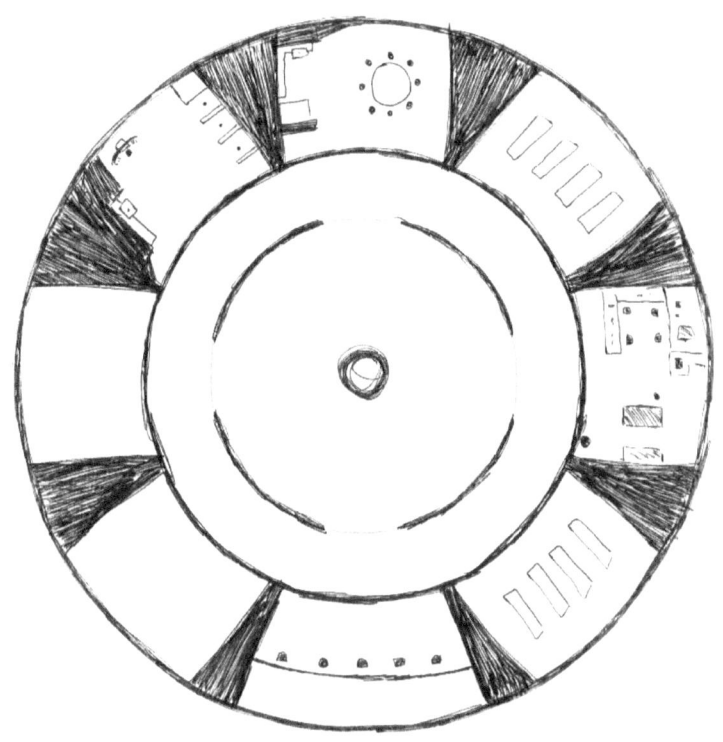

CHAPTER SEVEN: THE VIVARIUM

Gil Sanders was not the kind of man who had to shave every day in order to look presentable. He was also not the kind of man who could ever look presentable if he allowed himself to grow anything that could be defined as a beard. Gil's facial hair was just sporadic enough that, instead of growing into a thick beard, it would resemble the jowls of a stray dog if not taken care of soon enough. So he'd gotten pretty good at determining how many days it'd been since his last shave by simply touching his face. It took him roughly two days to get his five o'clock shadow, and after another two, Gil would look homeless. Thus, the third night, when his facial hair would transition from sandpaper to fuzz, was the sweet spot.

Stroking his face now, he guessed it must have been seven days since his hosts brought him aboard. He'd never before grown his facial hair out for seven days, but he supposed he'd likely be refused service at a fancy restaurant with a face like the one he wore now.

 This also marked somewhere around the fifth day Gil had spent locked in the circular chamber that was his holding cell—ever since Korben's unexpected dismemberment, Gil hadn't stepped foot out of the center room. That meant somewhere around five days without entering the exam room, five days without sneaking a sponge bath, and five days of completely raw mystery meat.

Until the morning of the fifth prison day, Gil hadn't really considered trying to sneak out of the chamber again—the thought didn't have enough time to gestate into anything more than a passing whim, because he'd always lift up his head to look around and see Korben. The giant had planted itself on what looked like a backless drum throne just behind the window of the center chamber closest to the kitchen, and stared at Gil as if it were a prison guard. It had a thick plate of dried and cracked clay on its back. To Gil's knowledge, Korben had not abandoned its post for even a moment until the start of the fifth waking period, which Gil had come to count as a span of time where the lights in the center room were turned on.

By the fifth waking period after the incident, Korben's lost arm had grown back to the elbow. The terminating point looked like a gnarled mass of raw biscuit dough, but it was infinitely less horrible to behold than the day after it had been severed.

When Gil woke up for the first time after being beaten unconscious with Korben's severed arm, he hadn't noticed right away that he was being watched. The first thing he did was touch his face and, that being the third waking period, he confirmed for himself the periods were comparable to twenty-four-hour days—it was time to shave. He was also acutely distressed to find several shards of the shattered plate embedded in his cheeks and forehead.

Wincing, he delicately pinched each piece, one by one, and tugged them out of his skin. They were incredibly small, not much bigger in thickness or length than the pin of a thumb tack, but they stuck in his skin like barbs and opened fresh, stinging wounds. Even in his pain, he produced a smile—he'd grown accustomed to tempered glass, which would safely shatter into harmless bits of smooth gravel if it broke.

There were also things like his garage door, which would all but mutter, "pardon me," and retreat back to the ceiling if it so much as bonked him on the head.

In contrast, provided the plate was a good representative, the sliding glass panes surrounding him could very well explode into a pile of needles if one of them should ever break. And forget about changing the door's mind if it'd had a notion to slide shut—it cut clear through Korben's arm like it was made of butter. Then again, if appendages could be lost without any sign of pain or even stress, he supposed safety wouldn't be such a big concern on Earth either.

It was when Gil's stomach rumbled that he looked up for the first time and spotted Korben. It sat on its stool with knees spread apart and right arm dangling between them. At this early point in time, its newly-severed arm still ended just below the shoulder, and didn't so much scab over as much as it just looked like sundried meat. The color, muted green interwoven with pale grey strands, was revolting to look at. The sight didn't ruin Gil's appetite, however. He'd gotten used to feeling hungry since boarding the ship, having only eaten a cumulative couple of fillets in as many days, but now he was ravenous.

Slowly making his way to his feet, Gil peed near the center of the room and watched it flow to the growing ecosystem he had pooling in the center. The disc above it perpetually warmed the mess like a heat lamp, keeping the stench strong and almost as awful as the aliens' own particular brand. He then walked over to the window where Korben stood watch. The alien's eyes rose to greet him, but it otherwise didn't move.

"Hey," Gil said flatly, eyelids half shut. "Sorry about your arm." He weakly gestured with his eyes to Korben's wound. "No hard feelings, right? Hey, can you slip me another plate of that mystery meat?"

There was no response, of course, verbal or otherwise.

"Come on, man, I gotta eat. I need something to drink too." Gil mimed inserting something into his mouth and then chewed.

But again, there was no response.

Looking closely at Korben, Gil was suddenly overcome with an inexplicable sense of shame. Like a bad dog—like a clumsy mutt brought inside that proceeded to piss on the carpet and chew everything up. Gil had inadvertently slapped that tall and skinny thing in the eye, was responsible for it getting its arm cut off, and had otherwise done nothing else but eat their food and urinate all over the floor. The feeling that Korben wanted to have him put down—to bring him out back and pump a few rounds into his head like he was some sort of rabid animal—played a large part in the imagery.

After almost a minute of continued staring, Gil's exhausted eyes went out of focus and he saw his own reflection in the window. His attention shifted to his eyes, which were surrounded with bruises—he had two black eyes. In the partial transparency of the window's reflection, it looked almost like he had no eyes at all—just two large and dark voids. He looked like one of them, and he could only giggle at the sight of himself.

"Hey look," he said in a deadpan tone, pointing to his black eyes with both hands, "I look just like you now. We're basically twins... right? You're not gonna let your brother starve to death, are you?"

After more silence, he put a hand on his stomach to really drive the point home. Even if they couldn't talk to each other, Gil knew Korben understood—it had given Gil its first meal aboard the ship with far fewer hints. Korben briefly glanced down at the gesture, and then returned its gaze to its previous position.

Gil's smile faltered, and after a moment, he scowled. "Look, I know what you guys are trying to do here. You think I'm stupid, but I'm pretty sure I got it figured out. You brought your Mayflower over here and we gave you some kinda Earth cold or something, and now you're trying to concoct a remedy." He tittered. "Well, if you don't give me something to eat, I'm gonna starve and you're all gonna look like dried-up pieces of old white *dog shit* until you drop dead." With only more silence as a response, Gil lost his temper. He shouted, "I NEED SOME FOOD!" and with every word, he slammed his open palms against the glass for effect. But when Korben finally stood up to challenge him, Gil caught another glimpse of the detail inside the thing's eyes and lost his nerve in an instant. It was just too terrible to look at.

He slowly backed up with his hands raised chest high in surrender, and returned to the center of the room. Korben took its seat again, and after a few moments of aimless pacing, Gil lay down with his back against the warm disc and fell asleep.

When he awoke again, roused by hunger, the lights were off. His hands were in front of his face and, as secretively as he could, he spread his fingers to look at the window across the room. From this vantage point, he could only see Korben's feet, but that was enough for him—he forced his eyes shut and eventually drifted back to sleep.

On the fourth waking period, Gil awoke with a start at the sound of something skidding along the floor towards his face. He lurched backwards instinctively, stopping inches away from the spinning disc behind him, and saw that his attacker was a dinner plate—he'd finally been granted a small meal. He never thought he'd be so happy to see a dish of raw meat.

Looking up, he saw Roger in the open doorway setting down a glass of water. It had to step around Korben, who had awkwardly held its ground as Roger maneuvered through the corridor and into the center room. With the glass of water safely on the floor, Roger slipped back though the threshold, slid the window shut, and disappeared.

Gil rose to his feet, walked to the window, snatched up the water, and looked down at the floor as he returned to his pathetic campfire. He greedily ate most of his meal by the handful, and then gulped his water down. With just a single sip remaining, he poured it into his palm and then scrubbed his hands together in an effort to dilute the sticky meat juices. Only a few small cubes of meat remained on the plate.

Far from sated, but no longer starving, Gil sat cross-legged on the ground with his mouth hanging open, and stared blankly at the spinning disc in the center of the room. He'd gotten so used to its perpetual hum he could hardly hear it. *What is that thing?* he wondered. The hatch underneath it was almost certainly how he came aboard, but because it was just a hole, it couldn't have been what pulled him upwards. So that meant either the spinning disc or the avant-garde chandelier on the ceiling had to be the culprit.

Gil lazily tossed one of his remaining meat cubes onto the spinning disc like an old man feeding bread to ducks at a park. He'd been curious since the day he arrived what would happen if he were to touch it, and raw meat would be an adequate test subject in the place of his finger. He also suddenly had a hope the disc would be hot enough to cook the meat. It would spell a grateful end for his raw meals. But when the cube made contact with the disc, it shot right back and flicked him square in the forehead.

The impact made Gil's eyes twitch involuntarily. It took him a moment to understand what had happened. Mouth still hanging open, brow furrowed, he looked down into his lap and saw the tiny meat cube between his legs. He rubbed his forehead—it hurt more than he thought it would—then picked the cube up and saw a corner had turned grey, which meant the disc was definitely hot enough to sear. But the thing was spinning so fast that using it as a frying pan was out of the question.

Okay, he thought, *so it's literally just a hot, spinning disc. So what's powering it? Is it self-powered? Perhaps it's powering the ship.* Gil didn't know. The disc might have been a solid piece of some unknown material, or stuffed full of foreign electronics. He shrugged.

Looking up, the chandelier caught his attention again. Like its counterpart hovering above the floor, it had to have a function but Gil didn't have the foggiest idea what it could be. He'd seen the disc float high into the air once before, and it was possible the chandelier was responsible for doing that. *Its job might be to hold the disc like a...* he pursed his lips for a moment, then snapped his fingers suddenly and said aloud, "containment field... or something." Then again, it was also possible it was a simple decoration—he just didn't know.

He took the same meat cube and chucked it high in the air. It hit one of the stalactites, dropped straight down, struck the disc, and flicked Gil on the forehead once again. He winced, then sighed. He glanced at Korben, who of course remained in its seat and stared.

"You gonna watch me twenty-four-seven?" he asked, knowing he'd get no response. And Korben did sit there and stare, as it would continue to do for the following two days. Gil assumed Korben was keeping watch for two reasons. First, Korben wanted to make sure Gil didn't sneak out of the center room again. Second, and more importantly, Gil had a feeling Korben didn't know *how* he got out of the center room, and was hoping he would try it again.

Both of these assumptions were correct—Korben *didn't* know how Gil managed to use their interface and skitter through the ship while they slept, and it *was* hoping to catch him in the act of another attempt. But there was also another reason, one which Gil hadn't considered: Korben was passing the time. Without any orders, it simply sat and stared at their captive, biding its time until the one in charge returned to the ship. And when their mission was complete—if they could in fact complete it—Korben had decided Gil was going to die whether the rest of the crew liked it or not. Until then, the giant would patiently wait and study its eventual victim.

After hours of aimlessly pacing around the room, punctuated by the occasional break to pee towards the dip in the center, the lights went dim. Gil lay down again and went to sleep.

He was startled from sleep again on the fifth day, when the humming of the orange disc suddenly intensified. His eyes darted to the center of the room where they grew wide with panic, and then a second later he was on his feet and sprinting to a window where Jeltz stood fiddling with something obscured by the adjacent panel. He pounded his fists against the sliding glass door and screamed rapid-fire questions at the poker-faced alien, namely, why was the disc rising? Were they going to blow him out into space? Why now?

Gil received no answers, of course, but he didn't have to wait long for a satisfactory response. As soon as the disc reached a height of about eight feet, the window behind Gil slid open. Roger awkwardly maneuvered around the stoic Korben and entered the center room. It was holding a device that looked... *nothing* like a vacuum cleaner, yet that's apparently what it was—Roger was here to clean up the area Gil had been using as a toilet.

Gil felt like all three of the aliens frowned slightly during this process. They had seen—or really, *watched*—him urinate many times, but no one aboard the ship save for Gil knew quite what to make of his feces. Gil had only done it the first night after eating the raw mystery meat, and mixed with the other fluids, the lava lamp contents looked a little unfamiliar even to him. And again, the otherworldly heat lamp didn't do the sludge any favors.

Their subtle expressions of confusion and disgust made Gil feel slightly embarrassed. He knew it smelled unpleasant, but the standard stench on these bozos was so terrible that his leavings should have hit them like potpourri. "What are you doing that for? Why not just blow it out?" he asked Roger. He didn't understand why they wouldn't just pull him out of the room for a moment and open the hatch to send it all out into space.

Roger shot him a look that reminded Gil of the animals from the old Flintstones cartoons—small animals repurposed as tools for menial tasks like mowing the lawn or playing the role of a garbage disposal. The alien gathered up a small sample of Gil's leavings, and then sucked up the rest in its vacuum. The alien had to get on its hands and knees to use it, a spongy-looking brick attached to a metal handle. It was so small Gil wasn't sure if it sucked it up or simply vaporized it. As Roger left, it collected Gil's dishes from the previous day and replaced them with a fresh meal. Gil didn't wait long to eat it.

That was the only direct interaction Gil had with his captors that day, although he saw a lot of them. All four of the center room's doors had opened, giving Gil four wide windows to stare out of as Roger and Jeltz marched through the corridors. Before long, Gil realized his makeshift toilet was just the first order of business. They were cleaning up the whole ship. All eight of the chambers were opened, which intrigued Gil; before that point, all of the chambers' shutters would slide back into place as soon as they were empty. Now it was as if they all had doorstops in front of them. He had a clear view of the cockpit, the exam room, the kitchen—obscured slightly by Korben—and a room Gil had previously never seen.

Midway between both the cockpit and kitchen windows, Gil saw a room where several spacesuits lined the wall on the left and what looked like a sliding escape hatch rested in the ceiling on the right. On the floor below it sat a small set of stairs, which looked to have bloomed smoothly from the seamless dark grey metal interior. It resembled the inside of an outdoor basement entrance. To Gil's surprise, this hatch was surrounded by a thin band of yellow, as if in warning. But on this ship, where doors cut through limbs and glass would shatter like a firework on impact, Gil still had a feeling he could simply grip the hatch's handle and painlessly slide it open without any resistance or triggered alarms.

The spacesuits looked ridiculous, mostly because of the creatures' generally long-and-skinny body shape. They were bright yellow, save for the beige boots and gloves, and were topped with obnoxiously-large fishbowl helmets. Gil thought they looked like the inflatable air dancers they always had at used car dealerships. He once again considered how he might blow his captors out into space, this time invoking one of his favorite movies where the protagonist donned a spacesuit and opened the door to get rid of her alien stowaway. But there was no way he'd ever fit into one of those lanky suits.

In the center of the room, between the suits and the exit, there was a simple rack with several long, clear poles jutting upwards. They each rested in a slot like pool cues on a billiard rack. In fact, their girth was similar to that of a pool cue, but they were roughly half as long and terminated in a sharp point. Gil thought they looked like glistening ice sculptures of pike spears, but couldn't determine what they might be used for. If they were made of metal, then they could certainly pass as weapons; but who would use a spear made of glass? Perhaps they weren't weapons, but tools of some sort?

Gil consulted his mental map. He remembered the showers were to the right of this room, but he never got a chance to see the room to the left. He cursed himself for lingering in the cockpit as long as he had—despite the terrible unfamiliarity of his surroundings and captors, he couldn't deny that he was also fascinated by how bizarre everything was. He pressed the side of his face against the glass and looked until his eyes felt strained, but still couldn't make out what was in that room. So he gave up and walked to the kitchen window.

Jeltz was putting dishes away, which made Gil smile. These creatures were usually the subject of horror movies—hiding in trees or peering through windows—so seeing aliens do mundane chores was a comically odd sight. Behind Gil, Roger was in the cockpit vacuuming up the shards of glass from the plate Gil had used to shield himself. He was surprised the mess hadn't been cleaned up before. *What have they been doing all day?*

Continuing to map the ship, Gil listed off the rooms he knew of starting with the room on his left. There were the showers, followed by the kitchen, the beds, the exam room, the extra beds, the cockpit, the mystery room, and finally, the newly observed exit route. The only thing Gil could imagine might be in the mystery room were supplies. *Probably stockpiles of that weird meat and a dozen tanks of drinking water*, he thought. It was just a guess though; like many other aspects of this ship and its owners, Gil just didn't know.

As he turned to observe Roger cleaning up the exam room—he couldn't believe Kif's mess still hadn't been mopped up—he caught a glimpse of Korben's arm, which had grown back to about halfway down its bicep. He did a double-take, and had to ask himself if that was where the arm had been severed; but no, he was sure it was just below the shoulder. He couldn't forget that if he tried. He pressed his face against the glass like a child peering out a car window.

"It's growing back," he deadpanned, then sighed. "Of course y'all aren't worried about safety. Why would you be?"

Gil was not at all surprised when Korben didn't respond. In fact, in just a few short days, he'd actually gotten quite used to having these one-way conversations. Just short of talking to himself, his interactions with his captors were often similar to how a man on a deserted island might confide in a coconut.

"You know, aside from the arm thing, I really don't see what your beef is with me. And it's growing back anyway." Then Gil was off to the window outside the cockpit, where he watched Roger like a spectator at the zoo.

Gil woke up peacefully the next day, on his side with his face resting on slightly sticky hands. Three of the windows were closed again, leaving Korben's stakeout near the kitchen as the only remaining view beyond the center room. Roger and Jeltz were in the kitchen, eating yet another meal of pink cubes. When they were finished, they brought two plates and two glasses to Korben, and then walked out of sight to do whatever it was they were going to do that day. From a distance, Gil waited for the window to slide open so he could receive his ration.

With a plate on its lap, Korben slowly worked its way through its meal, one cube at a time, stopping every now and then to take a sip from one of the odd white glasses resembling the end of a flute. If the alien was trying to be subtle by withholding Gil's meal, it failed—Gil was very familiar with this apparently universal behavior, and it was called 'being a dick.' When Korben was finished, it set down the empty plate, fiddled with the side of the door, and finally picked up the meal intended for Gil as the window slid open. It held the plate in its outstretched arm for Gil to take, scooting the cup past the threshold with its foot.

Gil waited for a moment, conflicted. He'd had the nerve to scream and pound his fists when there was a sheet of glass between them, but without a barrier, the giant terrified him. He felt pretty confident Korben wouldn't kill him, at least not with the others around, but Korben hadn't exactly been shy about inflicting any number of nonlethal injuries on Gil.

On the other hand, these beings had become almost completely demystified over the past few days. Their appearance—and especially those eyes—would certainly follow Gil's dreams for the rest of his life, but these were not the supernatural beings so many countless wackos claimed them to be. Instead, they were just sociopaths... rough, clumsy, stubborn, apathetic sociopaths. Gil took a deep breath, approached Korben, and took his meal without issue.

"How long are you gonna keep me in here, huh? When are you

going to take me home? *Are* you going to take me home?" Gil asked several rhetorical questions like this. Because he had no idea the aliens were waiting on someone to continue their work—all Gil knew was that this was his fourth day locked in a round room—he'd started to get the idea the ship had left the cover of The Moon to return back to wherever they came from. They were unable to complete their objective and safely return him home, so now they'd let everyone else take a shot. He hated the thought—being pulled apart in a foreign world's massive operating theater—but he couldn't see any other reason why he remained aboard the ship. If they were going to do something to him, why not just do it? If they weren't, why not take him home... or just get it over with and kill him?

He reluctantly returned to the center of the room and consumed his small meal. Several days of that raw meat had left him with an almost unbearable taste in his mouth. Each time he woke up, his saliva would be thick and foul. His morning breath was tinged with the taste of raw meat stuck between his teeth. When he finished his portion, he took the last sip of water into his mouth, swished it around for a while like mouthwash, and spat it back into his cup. He stared at the murky water for a moment, considered, and then drank that too.

With nothing else to look forward to for the day, Gil pondered his fate until the lights went out, and fell asleep.

Hours later, Gil awoke suddenly to the sound of a loud crash somewhere outside the center room. He shook his head to get his bearings and listened intently. He held his breath, and after a moment, he could hear light footfalls—multiple pairs of feet scurrying around a different part of the corridor. Gil thought this was odd. He remembered that he'd heard Korben stomping around when he first met them, but this was otherwise the only time he'd heard them through the walls. And so loudly... they must have been running around out there. The dim orange glow sill tinted the room. For lack of a better way to put it, Gil thought it must still be the middle of the night. He turned around to face the only window. Korben was gone. Gil's brow furrowed in confusion as he rose to his feet and walked over to the window.

Hands pressed against the glass, Gil peered out into the corridor. He continued to hear footsteps pounding around him, but saw nothing until either Roger or Jeltz caused Gil to gasp and jump back with a start as it abruptly sprinted past the window in a panic—at that speed, they were too similar in height for Gil to be able to tell the difference.

The footfalls stopped suddenly and reversed direction. It approached the window, but Gil saw only a portion of its face peek at him from the edge. A second later, a panel slid shut over the window, and the footsteps resumed around the corridor.

What the hell is going on out there? Gil thought. The sound of footsteps continued for some time, along with the occasional voice— never words, just exclamations—and Gil eventually followed the commotion to an area close to the mystery room. He pressed his face to the panel closest to the room, which didn't help. And then, just as suddenly as he'd been jerked from sleep, the commotion ceased. Once again, all he heard was the hum of the strange disc.

The overhead lights flickered on—whatever had happened, it was nearly the end of the night cycle anyway. He stared blankly at the wall for a few minutes, intensely curious, and then finally gave up.

After a moment's hesitation, he set his fists to the wall and started rubbing. The touchscreen came to life quicker than he expected. He didn't feel ill, but wondered if he maybe had a fever. He touched the option he hadn't chosen last time, which slid the panel out of the way but kept the window in place.

They all turned around to face him, and Gil shouted in surprise. Korben, tall as ever, stood with its severed arm now terminating at the elbow. Jeltz and Roger stood at its side. But behind them, another alien stood, covered in thick smears of bright red blood. And despite how similar they all looked, he swore the bloody one was Kif.

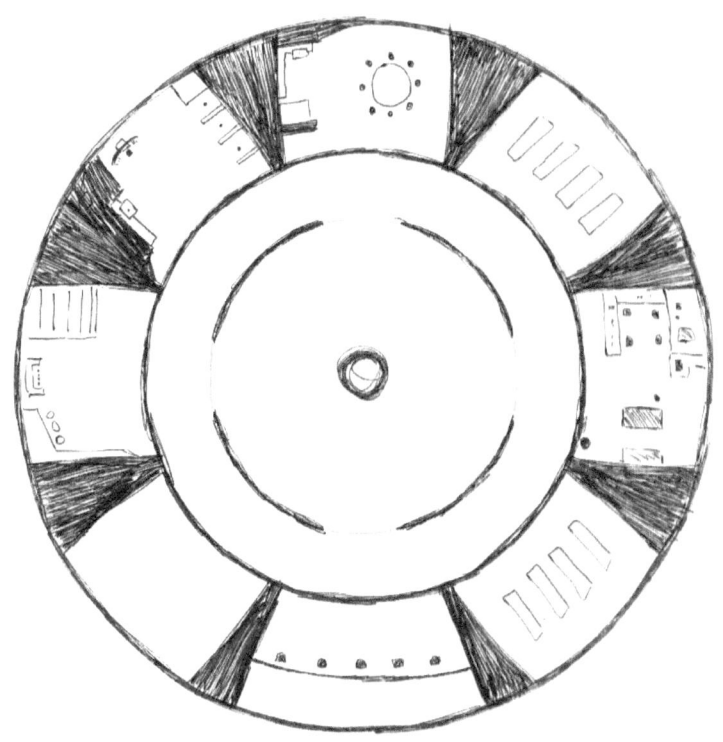

CHAPTER EIGHT: THE NEWCOMER

A wide-eyed Gil pointed both of his index fingers at the bloody alien and stammered, trying to make sense of what he saw. He'd personally witnessed the creature's execution and subsequent ejection into space. Its eyes had popped out of that bulbous head like a couple of champagne bottle corks and then splattered against the edge of the void like rotten fruit. Yet there it stood, same height, same timid gaze—unmistakably Kif. Or was it? Gil's mouth worked for a moment, but the only thing he could force out was an abrupt shout.

The aliens and Gil continued to stare at each other with shared surprise—their surprise that Gil had once again interacted with their foreign technology, and his surprise that they could apparently bring their own back from the dead. Or, no, that wasn't right; they *materialized* the thing back from the dead.

After more stammering, Gil simply shouted, "No!" as if

reprimanding a small child. He screamed the word at least a dozen times more, the syllable popping out of his mouth in staccato bursts like a dribbling basketball.

They turned away and walked towards the showers. Gil pounded on the window a few times in an unsuccessful attempt to have them come back, and then rested his face against the glass. A droning whine escaped him. He slowly backed up, navigating around the orange disc, and crouched with his back against the wall on the opposite side of the room.

Couldn't be, he thought. *I must have misplaced the commotion—it must have come in through the hatch I saw day before yesterday. They were standing in front of that room! But where did all that blood come from?* Korben's dismemberment had replayed in Gil's head a hundred times, and he recalled with crystal clarity that the wound hardly bled at all. But more importantly, the blood hadn't even been red; it was a pale grey with the slightest hint of green.

Maybe it wasn't blood. Maybe it was some sort of goop they hibernate in during space travel. It had to have come here in some sort of shuttle... maybe it's attached to the side of the ship... maybe it was discarded and crashed into The Moon. No... no way—it's not Kif, it's just Kif's replacement. Gil had to admit he'd mostly been able to distinguish them by height alone—line up their faces, and it was like trying to differentiate between four ants on an ant hill. There were only the slightest of differences.

Korben's eyes always looked a bit angrier. Its hairless eyebrows always seemed to be angled downwards towards its nostrils. Then there was Jeltz, whose brow seemed permanently furrowed and whose lips seemed to curl downwards at the corners in a subtle frown—it looked pompous. Roger and Kif, however, just looked blank. For the most part, they were all nearly identical.

He'd convinced himself the new alien couldn't be Kif. He recalled the old trope where Junior's goldfish dies, but mom and dad flush it down the toilet and buy a new one while he sleeps. When Junior wakes up, he has no idea it's a different fish. Gil just happened to have the insider knowledge of seeing the fish go down the toilet.

Gil calmed down a bit and reminded himself that the aliens were not supernatural. He was still distressed that they had apparently invited company over, but comforted that it couldn't possibly have been the late Kif. *But why is it here?* he wondered.

The paneled wall behind Gil suddenly recessed a bit and then started to slide behind another panel. He quickly lurched forward, springing to his feet and whirling around to see his captors as the window slid open as well. The exam room was open behind them. The quartet stood in the corridor, just as they had when he'd first met them. Then the shortest of them, now clean, beckoned to Gil with its index finger. The thing was using hand gestures—a form of communication that Kif had obviously learned through contact with him. Despite this, Gil insisted in his mind that it had to be a different alien.

Gil considered going to them, then shook his head. "No way—you guys wanna play doctor again? What more do you need? You've already taken a sample of damn-near everything my body makes. Please, just—please don't. I don't want to go back in there."

He didn't move until Korben impatiently started towards him. He quickly lifted his hands in front of himself, insisting, "Okay, I'm coming, I'm coming," but he had misunderstood—they didn't need him to go into the exam room. Korben reached him and merely hooked its right arm under Gil's left shoulder. Then Jeltz approached and did the same thing to his right. They held him in place. Neither of them gripped with any amount of real force, but that was somehow worse for Gil than being violently pushed around.

The stench had come back worse than ever before, filling his nostrils with the reek of fetid sweat and old fish. Their bodies were lightly pressed against his, and the hands cupped under his arms rested on his shoulders in a sort of caress. It was unbearable, like standing on a crowded subway train, sandwiched between two warm, naked corpses. Gil wriggled in discomfort.

With the two aliens holding him, Roger walked into the exam room and returned a moment later with a fresh syringe.

"What are you going to—" Gil began, but winced before he could finish. Roger approached his left arm—the arm not already decorated with a dozen needlepoint wounds—and ungracefully pounded the needle into the space just below his elbow. Gil looked down at the source of the pain and whined loudly, his mouth hanging open in a frown like a tragic theater mask. The aliens' grip around his shoulders tightened a bit, which was preferable to the dry warmth of their soft touch. His high-pitched exhales continued rhythmically until Roger completed the draw and ripped the needle back out—the alien was two-for-two now. Bedside manner aside, Roger had successfully completed a procedure on the first attempt.

With the fresh sample in hand, Roger turned around and walked towards the exam room. The two aliens released Gil and followed suit, with the newcomer trailing behind and fidgeting with some controls outside the center room. The window slid shut again, and the other three panels in the room slid open to reveal their own windows. Then all the teeth of the cog opened up simultaneously, once again giving Gil a view of most of the ship. Gil put pressure on the hole in his left arm to stop the flow of blood. When he returned his attention to the quartet, they were all in the exam room.

Gil was more than a little perplexed. They apparently only needed a blood sample from him this time, and therefore didn't think it necessary to keep him strapped down on the exam table, but why the sudden transparency? Why open all the doors and let the lab rat observe? He supposed it was possible they wanted to ease his mind—to show him he wasn't there just to be tortured, but so they could work something out. He of course wasn't sure if this was really the intent, but Gil admitted to himself it was certainly the effect.

The gesture also added some credibility to his idea that they were sick. They didn't want to tear him apart; they just wanted to save their skins. Kif had obviously bungled the first attempt when it injected itself with whatever goop it cooked up, so the newcomer had to be the replacement, here to take another crack at things. Yes, it might have just been vain hope, but Gil did see this as an attempt to make him feel more comfortable.

I think I'd feel a lot more comfortable if you locked up the big one, he thought. It was crystal clear at this point that Korben was the only one of them who treated Gil with hostility. The others weren't exactly good hosts, but Korben was on another level entirely. Granted, Gil had played a large part in the loss of Korben's arm, but that event hadn't exactly been the trigger for its attitude.

As usual, Korben sat at the entrance to the exam room on the same seat he'd occupied when monitoring Gil the past few days. Roger and the Kif—no, the newcomer— sat at a counter topped with various assembled technologies and went straight to work. The new blood sample was pumped into a slender tube atop a device not too dissimilar in appearance from a top-loading inkjet printer. It was roughly the size of a shoebox, with a small cavity in the center and a slender tray jutting out the bottom.

All of the technological components stood out from the furniture and walls of the ship. Unlike the rough hematite finish covering all the interior surfaces, the components had a brushed nickel finish similar to the chandelier in the center chamber.

The newcomer produced another syringe and jabbed it into its forearm with only the slightest flinch of pain. Gil stared at the procedure with his open hands against the glass until Jeltz, who had previously stood next to the two seated aliens, walked out of the exam room and down the corridor to the right. Curious, Gil followed along from inside the center room to see where it was headed. The haughty-looking alien stopped in between the windows leading to the cockpit and exit chambers, which meant the mystery room was its destination. Gil couldn't see what was happening—the room wasn't in view of his prison cell. But after another moment, it headed back towards the exam room holding a steaming, translucent white cube in its hands. It was a cube of ice, Gil realized, each side measuring roughly four inches in length, with a small mass in the center.

"What is that?" Gil asked rhetorically, the unmistakable tone of fascination in his voice. He followed Jeltz along the wall and stopped at the window outside the exam room, where the alien returned and deposited the cube into a small device—also cubic, and seemingly just large enough to contain the frozen chunk.

Then the newcomer finally withdrew the syringe from its arm. Gil could hardly see it from the distance he stood from—about ten feet—but near the bottom of the upturned syringe sat a small globule of what he recognized from Korben's wound to be alien blood. He only saw a hint of it. It had to have been less than a teaspoon, which meant withdrawing it must have been tantamount to sucking tar through a coffee stirrer.

The newcomer inserted the syringe's needle into the same tube Gil's blood had been pumped into, and ejected the sludgy substance. Then it and Roger were off, their nimble fingers tapping away on the screens at the counter. A flurry of typed gibberish fluttered onto one end of their displays and scrolled away on the other—the distinctive look of data entry.

Jeltz used a pair of tongs to reach into the cubic device and retrieve the small, dripping mass that had been at the center of the now-melted piece of ice. It was roughly the size of a robin egg, grey in color, and apparently fragile judging by the care the alien took in handling it. It seemed almost to jiggle under the timid pressure of Jeltz's tongs. The small object was placed inside the front cavity of the printer lookalike, and in an instant, needles coming from several different directions within the device plunged into it. Roger and the newcomer continued to type away at their touch displays.

Stuck in his holding cell, Gil periodically grew bored in the ensuing hours, passing the time by circling the room, talking to himself, or occasionally sitting cross-legged and simply rocking back and forth. He watched Jeltz return to the mystery room several times to retrieve more ice cubes—he counted four trips all together—but they otherwise all stayed in the exam room. He wished he could get out of that round room—to be near them and see what they were doing, or see what was in that one room Gil hadn't been able to see yet. Instead, he felt like he was stuck in a crows nest at the top of a large boat, or a child stuck at the bottom of a well. He looked up into the chamber for no particular reason at one point as Korben got up from its seat and joined the other three at the counter.

Déjà vu, Gil thought. And sure enough, the newcomer just happened to be pulling the syringe out of its chest just as Kif had done before. Gil chuckled in disbelief, but his half-smile quickly curdled into a shocked frown when Korben refilled the syringe and stabbed its own chest with it. One by one, all four of them took a syringe full of the new concoction straight to the chest. Aside from most subtle wince of pain, they each took the shot without issue. On the counter, Gil saw a grey mass in the printer lookalike, and three other gelatinous masses off to the side which were... anything but grey. An unappetizing mixture of white, green, and black speckled the discarded lumps.

"I sure hope you know what you're doing this time," Gil shouted through the window. His voice, muffled through the sheet of glass, visibly surprised them as if they'd forgotten he was there, and it made Gil look sideways at them. They were quite good at ignoring Gil, but when he surprised them, it was almost as if they broke character and forgot to pretend they were deaf. It reminded him of visiting old relatives in nursing homes. When the nurses came in to check up, some of the elderly patients were so far gone that the easiest way to deal with them as they thrashed and wailed in their beds was to pretend they weren't speaking at all.

Korben left the other three and walked to the window, where it lifted its hand and fiddled with what was surely one of the phantom touch displays. A moment later, all four windows were concealed by their panels, and Gil was once again alone in his circular holding cell.

Gil stood in stunned silence, confused by the sudden farewell from the quartet. He stammered for a moment, not sure how to react, but when the lights dimmed for the night, his eyes grew wide. He pounded his fists against the wall.

"Wait a minute!" he cried. "You never gave me anything to eat!" Gil continued pounding for a few moments, but it was no use. He wasn't sure if they'd gone to sleep, but he couldn't hear anything through the walls. He ultimately gave up and looked around his holding cell. It was just as it'd been the first night he'd arrived.

He lay down near the center of the room with his back to the spinning disk, but did not fall asleep—he was too hungry. *How could they forget to feed me?* They never gave Gil enough to eat as it was, so a skipped meal felt like torture.

He briefly considered opening the panel and sneaking out again for a cut of meat, but when it came down to it, he just didn't have the guts. If Korben were to catch him again, who knew what it would do to him. No, he decided it would be best to wait until morning. At that point, they'd surely open up a door and feed him, unless they'd all dropped dead from—

"Oh, God, what if they're all dead?" he whispered, eyes wide in the darkness. How could they know for sure the newcomer was more successful than Kif? What if all four of them had taken another faulty batch of ooze and croaked during the night? Experience had certainly shown him they were at least a little reckless. The thought of them all turning into corpses briefly excited Gil, but then terrified him—if they were all dead, how the hell was he going to get home? Even if he got the ship moving, which would be a miracle in its own right, there would still be the issue of steering, not to mention reentry into Earth's atmosphere, and the act of landing the damn thing. If he crashed into a body of water, would the ship sink? What if he crashed onto land? What if he crashed on land a million miles from home? Did the cockpit even have seatbelts?

Or what if more replacements showed up? What if they didn't show up until Gil had already gotten the ship moving? Would they board the saucer and drag him back behind The Moon?

Gil didn't have an answer for any of these questions.

Thoughts of starving to death or eventually suffocating might have kept Gil awake all night if they'd had the theater of his mind to themselves, but these fears eventually received the vaudeville hook. After hours of anxiously rocking back and forth on his side, he suddenly rolled forward involuntarily. He rolled over again and again, like a child would roll down a grassy hill, until finally bumping into the wall at the edge of the room. The force which continued to hold him against the wall was a familiar feeling to anyone who had ever entered a vehicle:

the ship had accelerated, and continued to do so. While he was relieved—this meant they couldn't all be dead—the sudden movement also terrified him.

"Where are we going?" he screamed. At this point, there wasn't even a sliver of hope for a response; like all his other verbiage of late, the question was rhetorical. But he was fairly certain his destination could only be one of two places: his home, or theirs.

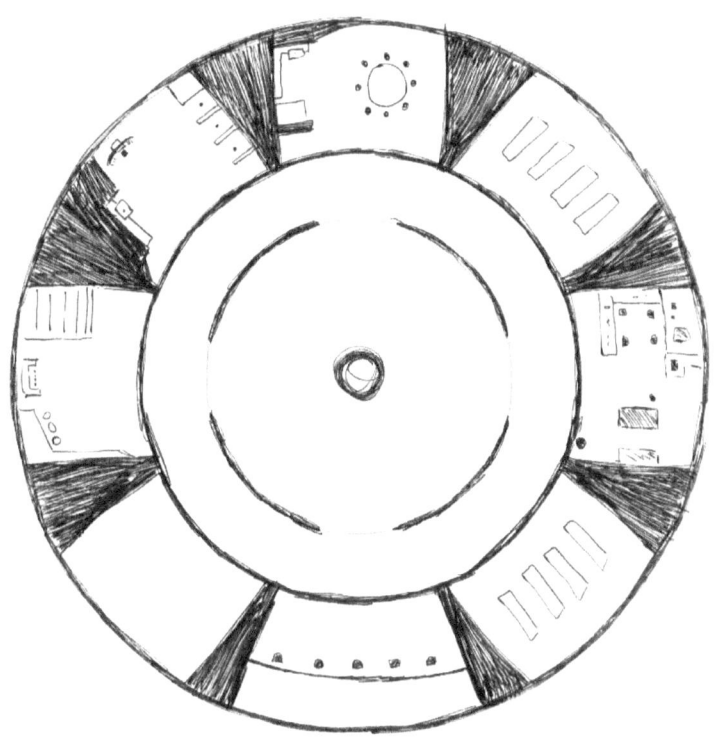

Chapter Nine: Positive Results

Gil was pulled from pseudo sleep when the lights in the round room flickered to life. God, was he thirsty. Hungry, too. He hadn't so much slept the previous night as much as he'd simply passed out from exhaustion.

Hours before, once the subtle force holding him against the wall faded away, he cautiously made his way back towards the center of the room. Lying down again, he had yet another fear to add to his steadily growing list: if the ship stopped suddenly, or accelerated in the opposite direction, he'd be sandwiched between his toilet and the hotplate. If he'd randomly chosen to make his bed on the other side of the disc, he would have been dead already. When he finally did calm down and approach something similar to sleep, it felt more like daydreaming. He'd gotten terrible rest, and wasn't ready to start a new day.

Did they turn the lights on? he wondered. *Or is it on some kind of timer?* He wasn't sure if they'd survived the night, but on cue, the panel closest to the cockpit slid away to reveal the quartet. Without even bothering to look up—his tired eyes caught a glimpse of four silhouettes, and that was all he needed—Gil got to his feet and shuffled towards them.

"It's about time," he slurred in a raspy and croaky voice, following up with questions about where they were taking him and whether or not he could finally have something to eat and drink.

He looked up a little and saw the newcomer was holding a plate of cubed meat and a glass of water. Roger was snacking on its own dwindling portion of cubes. A grateful smile spread across Gil's face as he looked higher up, but after his eyes focused on his captors, he stopped dead in his tracks. Something was different.

Finally living up to their eponymous nickname, their skin appeared grey, rubbery, and moist. It looked like the skin of a dolphin. Gil thought they still looked plenty hideous, but they also seemed to be healthier—much healthier, in fact. The newcomer, Jeltz, and Roger looked almost happy. And why not? Though there had been some bumps in the road, they had apparently succeeded in their mission to find a remedy for what was ailing them.

After a moment of confirmation, he let his eyes go back out of focus. He'd gotten rather good at staring past them, the way a person might pretend to be blind: he'd focus on something behind them, enough to reduce them to blurry, poorly-defined shapes. This was the most comfortable way for Gil to face them. He saw the cockpit was opened behind them, although the window panel was still closed.

"Where's the big one?" Gil asked. "Korben?" He was a little startled by his own question; it was the first time he'd uttered one of his assigned names out loud, and it made him chuckle. He was sure he'd seen four figures in the doorway before getting up, but Korben was nowhere in sight. He figured he must have been mistaken. "Well, I hope your friend is dead," he concluded flatly.

The window slid open, and the newcomer extended its arms with the meal in hand. Gil stepped forward, took the plate and glass, and then stepped back. Placing the glass of water in the crook of his arm, he wasted no time in eating, grabbing several cubes at a time with his free hand and shoving them into his mouth. Halfway through the meal, he took the glass of water with his sticky hand and turned it up, spilling every last drop into his mouth.

The newcomer spread out its arms, as if to proclaim, "Behold!"

Gil scoffed. "Yeah, I get it. I had a feeling you guys had caught something. I guess they don't have the common cold where you're from, but maybe you'll take some precautions and at least put on some damn clothes next time you wanna go exploring."

The newcomer continued to stare at Gil with a dull, almost imperceptible smile.

With a mouthful of meat, Gil sheepishly added, "I—I'm glad it worked out. When can I go home?" He knew that if the newcomer had attempted to answer that question in whatever way it could, it would have been simple coincidence. Without any way for them to understand each other, the alien's own will to take him home would have been the only thing to prompt a response.

The newcomer appeared to be initiating another gesture, but stopped abruptly as if something had suddenly grabbed its attention. With wide eyes, the newcomer pivoted to the left and looked up as Korben, whose footsteps were now conspicuously audible, came into view from the corridor and looked straight at Gil. And of course, Gil only briefly made eye contact before reverting back to his unfocused gaze.

Like its travel companions, Korben's skin had taken on a healthy and moist shade of grey. Its left arm had grown all the way back to the wrist, terminating in a small bulb. The others seemed agitated. The newcomer placed a hand on Korben's chest in a gentle command to stop, but Korben lifted its right arm and brushed the short alien aside.

Its right hand held something Gil recognized, but couldn't immediately place. It was a clear pole, a little over two feet long and ending in a sharp point. Gil looked sideways at the thing and then remembered after a moment it was one of the tools he'd seen in the exit chamber. Next, it became clear that Korben wasn't merely holding the object, but brandishing it as if it were a weapon. Finally, with dawning clarity as Korben drew the small spear backwards, Gil realized Korben meant to attack him.

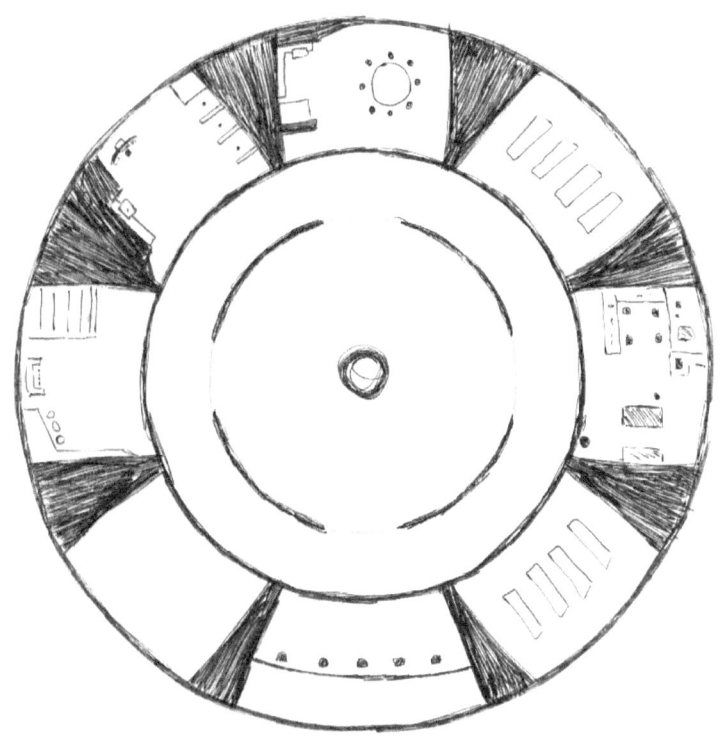

CHAPTER TEN: A SONG OF SIXPENCE

Gil's plate and cup clattered to the floor as he lunged backwards, narrowly escaping the impossibly sharp tip of the clear rod. Korben had assumed a stance that looked unfamiliar to Gil but was still clearly the result of some form of combat training: bent knees, one leg in front of the other, and the diminished left arm pointing behind Korben with the wielding arm up front.

Gil shouted, "Wait!" as he backed up, defensively holding his hands out in front of him. Korben stomped after him, swinging and thrusting like a crazed swordsman. Ever mindful of the spinning disc in the middle of the room, Gil navigated around it backwards while clumsily dodging the repeated thrusts of Korben's weapon. Several times, the tall one swung the object at Gil, content to simply crack him across the face with it like a club; but somehow, to Korben's visible frustration and Gil's sheer disbelief, the weapon hadn't managed to make contact.

Gil was already nearly out of breath, and running out of luck just as quickly. He hadn't been well rested to begin with, and his burst of adrenaline was draining fast. Would-be shouts of whys, waits, stops, and pleases came out in ragged exhales as he tried as hard as he could to avoid meeting the business end of Korben's spear. It was so obvious to him; of course, now that they'd gotten what they came for, the cat had decided to play with the mouse before killing it.

At last, the terrified Gil tripped over his own feet and fell onto his back. Korben moved between Gil's flailing legs, stepped its left food on his stomach, and towered over him. Its spear shot high up into the air, ready to finally land a blow and dispose of Gil.

The spear flew down like a bullet. With the last ounce of Gil's strength, he twisted his body to the right and just barely cleared the path of the weapon. It rang out with a deafening clang as the tip made contact with the floor of the round room, the sound sending sharp pain into Gil's ears. He feared they would begin bleeding. Korben roared with anger and drew the spear back again. Gil couldn't fight it anymore—his body refused to move. He watched helplessly as Korben's right arm came down a second time.

But just as the spear was about to drive into the soft tissue of Gil's side, Jeltz leaped up from behind Korben and grabbed the giant's shoulder. The force caused Korben to swing backwards, interrupting the spear's path and sending it across Gil's belly and up into the air like a pendulum. The swipe left only a slight abrasion; if Gil had been inhaling, he would have opened up like rubber coin purse.

Gil was stunned—the other alien appeared to be defending him. It became clear in an instant that Korben was acting alone.

The tall one shook Jeltz halfway off and then flung the alien away with its diminished left arm. Jeltz landed on the spinning disc—audibly slowing its rotation like a soft brake pad—and was then immediately and harshly thrown off. It hit the floor and rolled several times over, like a person thrown from a moving vehicle. The lights seemed to flicker for a moment, as if an engine somewhere had sputtered. Gil lifted his head slightly and saw that a portion of Jeltz's backside was seared, a small mess of dark grey and pale green. It barked in pain—in fact, Gil realized they all seemed to be barking. The short, staccato grunts of quarreling apes filled the room. Roger was now making its way towards Korben from the other side of the room, while the newcomer remained in the doorway and worriedly stared—

Gil once again heard the clang of the spear meeting the ground, and screamed in pain. His eyes shot to his left side, where he saw that the spear had grazed him. It left a slit not unlike the score a baker would cut into the top of a loaf of bread, and the pain intensified with each passing second. It burned—no, seared his insides as if they were being cauterized. He felt as if a jellyfish had burrowed into his flesh.

Gil batted the clear pole away and felt Korben falter like an old man whose cane was kicked out from under him. He looked up to see Korben's ugly face and, for the first and last time, he saw a smile. The giant's mouth looked like a grinning skull. It had bent over so far that its face was mere inches away from Gil's. It stood back up, lifted the spear over its head, and whacked the wound in Gil's side. He wailed in pain. He was unsure if the grazing stab had been poor aim or if Korben just wanted to toy with him, but he was relieved that it didn't seem to be fatal.

Roger finally reached Korben's right side and tried to restrain the giant. Korben, caught in the frenzy of finally doing away with Gil, shot its right hand back to forcefully push Roger away; but it accidentally plunged the sharp end of the spear through Roger's eye and into its brain. The point made an audible popping sound as it pierced the black orb, and again as it cracked through the other side leading to the grey matter. The skewered alien let out an abrupt and short, high-pitch shriek, and then fell backwards. The eye slid off the spear smoothly, like an olive pulled off a cocktail toothpick, and Roger hit the floor like a statue. It twitched, and then lay still.

For what felt like an eternity, the room was silent. All eyes were on Roger's corpse—even Gil's, who'd momentarily forgotten about the pain in his side. A panic-stricken Korben dropped the spear, which hit the ground with several sharp clangs before settling. The noise seemed to kick-start the clock back into motion—Jeltz suddenly cried out for its fallen companion, banging its fists on the ground. It was the most unpleasant sound Gil had ever heard in his life. It struggled to its feet, careful not to agitate the burn on its backside, and limped over to Roger. The newcomer followed suit, whining the whole time. They sat around the body, clearly mourning the loss. Gil was confused—when Kif died, they hadn't done much more than toss the body out the window. It had been as if an appliance stopped working and was then simply discarded. But around Roger, they reacted in a way Gil would *expect* someone to react when a close friend dies. *Poor Kif*, he thought. *I guess Roger was just more important.*

Korben took a few steps back, its face still wearing an expression of panicked anguish, and then darted for the opening that led to the corridor. The feeling of déjà vu rose up in Gil again, and despite everything, he started to laugh. With a voice long ago turned hoarse, the laughter tumbled out like a cackling witch. He hurt. The pain reasserted itself as the laughter continued, forcing him to hold his sides; but the more it hurt, the more uncontrollable the laughter became. The sandpaper in his throat finally interrupted, leading to hacking coughs and gasps for air, but the grimacing smile persisted.

He couldn't help it—he felt like he was watching a reenactment. And sure enough, the giant returned with the stout, mercy-killing device that it'd shoved through Kif's skull just a few days before. An all-new fit of laughter erupted from Gil. If he'd been able to speak, he would have asked the giant what the point was of mercy-killing a corpse—Roger was already dead. Instead, he continued to choke on his laughter. His initial opinion of them reasserted itself, and Gil thought, *God help them, they're just stupid kids in over their heads.*

The others attempted to shoo Korben away, but it forced past them. Just as before, Korben cleanly shunted the device into Roger's forehead. And just as before, the device lit up red and blared like a foghorn. Of course, there was no twitching this time, no creepy undulation from the lifeless alien. Gil, screaming with hoarse cackles, watched through blurry eyes and waited for the green light and single beep. But it never came.

With its right hand wrapped around the hilt of the device, Korben impatiently pounded its left nub on the floor of the round room. After a moment, the device's red light shut off, and blared its foghorn sound again. Gil stared at the three of them, lying on his stomach with his laughter finally under control. *This isn't in the script*, he thought. *It's supposed to turn green.*

The newcomer and Jeltz stood up and stared at Korben, who remained crouching at the head of the corpse. When it finally rose up and locked eyes with the other two aliens, it scowled and started towards them.   They each intercepted one of Korben's arms and restrained the giant, similar to how the they'd restrained Gil the day before. Korben barked in protest, falling backwards and slumping as the others dragged it out of the room. It fought hard, and could have easily overpowered any two men, but its travel companions managed to subdue the angry alien and take it away. Gil heard the commotion continue just outside the view of the door, which meant they were in the leftmost reaches of the cockpit. Straps were pulled, tones were shouted, and feet continued to stomp.

Gil was alone. His laughter had died as completely as his new roommate, and was replaced with a sense of confusion. Despite the similarities to the other day, things had taken a sudden turn. Was Korben in trouble for trying to murder Gil, or for accidentally killing Roger? Why would Korben try to put Roger out of its misery after it had clearly already died? And why didn't the device behave the same way as before?

He got to his feet and started towards Roger, but could barely manage. The pain in his side screamed. Contorting himself to get a good look, he moved his slashed shirt out of the way and saw what appeared to be processed ham. The spear, it seemed, hadn't so much cut into him as it had simply deleted what it touched. His side looked like the notch in the long end of a carnival ticket stub. And God, the throbbing pain.

He knelt down to pick up the spear. He looked closely, narrowing his eyes in an effort to see the finer details, and noticed a small hollow running along the inside of the glass rod. His eyes moved along the length of it to the tip, where more scrutiny revealed tiny pores. He looked back towards the other end of the spear and located a small button. Pressing the button pushed a clear substance through the pores of the spear's tip, like the clear sludge from a stick of deodorant. Lightly pressing the tip to the left leg of the corpse, he was horrified to see the spear melt through like butter. It had to be some sort of acid.

Gil cautiously set the spear on the floor again and looked Roger up and down. Its left hand had slipped under the spinning disc and rested in Gil's urine. He used his foot to scoot it out of the puddle, and then looked at Roger's face. "I'm sorry I named you Roger," he lamented. "I should have called you Zoidberg, or Phlox, or some other alien that'd had at least been a doctor and knew a thing or two about humans. Instead I named you after a jackass prima donna from a cartoon."

Beside the corpse's head was the thumbtack-shaped device they all seemed to favor for putting the final punctuation mark on a life. He thought about picking it up, but decided not to after seeing the flesh and blood pasted around the spike. He saw, however, that there was a small opening at the tip of the black spike and wondered what it could be used for. He'd assumed the device was just a simple thing that shocked them to death—like a portable electric chair—but maybe something was ejected through that small hole? Or maybe something was sucked up through the hole?

It occurred to him, suddenly, that if the cockpit was open, *all* of the outer chambers might be open. Perhaps it was time to see where this strange device came from. He started walking towards the center room's only open exit immediately, forgetting about his pain in an instant. He'd been wondering for days what might be in that final room, and with the trio occupied, this might be his only chance to find out.

He reached the threshold and cautiously peered out from the edge of the doorway. Korben was seated at the leftmost of the five chairs in the cockpit, strapped down with several seatbelts across its chest, waist, and lap. A few smaller straps held both arms in place at the biceps and wrists, which perplexed Gil—he wondered why a chair would ever need straps like that, unless they expected that they might need to restrain someone. The nub of Korben's diminished left hand was able to freely slide in and out of the loop formed by the strap, but that didn't seem to bother Jeltz or the newcomer. They sat across from Korben with their backs against the control board. All three of them stared at each other, no doubt engaged in one of their silent conversations. Gil crept to the right, excited to see that the mystery room was indeed open.

In the center of the room stood a column at a height of roughly four and a half feet. On the left, three dividers of similar height extended from the wall and floor—it had the same bloomed appearance as all the other permanent furniture on the ship, as well as the same glossy dark silver finish. Each divider was somewhere around seven feet long, collectively forming two stalls with five feet of width and seven feet of depth. Though Gil's focus was currently on the left side of the room, his peripheral vision revealed that the right wall held two identical stalls.

Both of the stalls on the left were empty, save for a small series of channels etched into the floor that led to a drain dead center. The drains were topped with little covers, making them resemble shower stalls. He could smell something—something familiar—but he couldn't quite put his finger on it. It was something like raw meat. And past the second stall, in the two-foot space between its wall and the tapered wall of the ship, Gil was relieved to see several clear crates of various shapes and sizes containing the picked-clean remains of cattle. Just... regular cattle; the source of the crew's food supply.

Each crate seemed to contain specific categories of remains. One crate held the bleached-white bones of appendages. One contained a heap of disassembled ribcages. Another was a disgusting mess of organs and tissue they'd apparently determined weren't fit for consumption. Underneath that was another crate stuffed full with skins. The topmost crate held four bovine skulls.

Four cows, he thought. *Either this quartet's been here a long time, or these things consume a lot more meat than they let on.* Gil knew that four cows had to have yielded something close to two thousand pounds of red meat. But judging by the refrigerator he'd recently gotten into, they didn't have more than a couple of steaks remaining.

Gil turned around to view the right side of the room and saw two identical stalls. One of them was just as empty as the others, while the final stall was *anything but* empty. A cow, dead, lay on its side with its belly ripped open. There had obviously been a lot of blood, but it'd collected in the channels leading to the drain, caking it like a layer of dark brown wax. He wondered for a moment why flies and maggots weren't already moving in and living off the land, then remembered where he was. *No insects out here.*

The cow's mouth had been outfitted with some sort of respirator that looked to have been there for weeks. Blood and saliva had at first coated the inside of the mask, then became cracked and discolored. The guts, on the other hand, looked no more than a day old. Yes, the blood was dried and drying, but the innards were still saturated with juices. Its torso was a mess. He was a little surprised to realize the thing didn't stink. He supposed its flesh hadn't sat long enough to rot, but cattle didn't smell pleasant when they were alive. Also, Gil never heard a peep from it, though he supposed it was possible the mouth piece had held it in some sort of coma.

A gigantic chunk had been ripped from its chest, leaving a cozy grotto behind numerous cracked and broken ribs. Some portions of its furry skin looked to have been sliced open with a sharp blade, while other portions bore the grooves of fingers. It was as if one of them had attempted to cut it up by the book, while the others were so hungry they'd ripped into it with their bare hands like zombies in a gritty horror movie. But why did so much meat remain? Hundreds of pounds of edible flesh stuck to its bones, simply going to waste.

Gil moved closer to get a better look and almost ran into the square column in the middle of the room. His attention shifted to a clear glass lid on top of the column, and he could see a few dozen ice cubes inside—some of the same cubes Jeltz had ushered to the exam room the day before. They were meticulously stacked to ensure there was no wasted space, but judging by the scratch marks along the inner walls, several dozen cubes had been removed over time. In fact, they seemed to be running low.

He opened the lid—it pulled upwards on hinges, like the top of a gas station barrel cooler, and a pleasant coolness wafted out at him from inside the hollow column. He bent down and attempted to pick up one of the cubes, but it was too cold; his sweaty fingers stuck to the dry surface, and when he pulled his hand back, he winced in pain as one of the heavy cubes came with him.

He closed the lid of the column, set his hand down, and carefully peeled his fingers off the ice. He lost a bit of skin, which stung, but he was otherwise fine. In the center of the cube, a small mass hung suspended. With his hands on his knees, he kneeled down slightly and peered inside to try to determine just what the hell was in there. But as the heat of the room settled into the surface of the ice, the foggy exterior melted away to a glossy sheen, and the cube slid into a square groove in the center of the lid. He hadn't noticed it before. The lid was slightly concave with a small groove in the center, each side measuring about four inches—like it was engraved specifically for the purpose of holding these cubes in place.

Gil found it difficult to make anything out under the wavy, optical tricks of the frozen water, but he eventually pieced together what the mass was: some sort of embryo. Two black eyes and four nubs protruding out of a grey slug formed a vaguely familiar chibi version of his captors. *This must be why they were successful the second time they injected themselves,* Gil thought. *They got it right by making several of these things their guinea pigs. I guess those discolored lumps on the counter had to have been failed attempts.* Gil found this to be strange, not to mention a little unethical, but even stranger was the question of why the numerous embryos shared the same space as the crew's food supply.

He shifted his focus to the column. Three of the column's sides were bare, but on its far side—the side closest to the tapered edge of the ship—he saw a single button and a shelf underneath containing five of the mercy-killing devices that'd been used on Kif and Roger. Each device sat attached to a base, and he saw enough room for two more of them. *Seven all together,* he thought, and of course knew why two were missing. *Why do they have so many of them?* Two of the five seemed to be completely powered down, while three had the same green light illuminating from the hilt he'd seen when Kif had been executed.

Gil brought his finger to the button above the shelf, hesitated for a moment, and then pressed it. A hatch in the ceiling slid open, and a claw on a multi-elbowed metal arm emerged. The claw looked like a thing people would waste quarters on trying to grab a stuffed animal at an arcade. It straightened its many joints, extending down to the lid of the column, and gripped the ice cube. The claws then spun around the cube, shaving it down and shooting ice chips everywhere until only a small chunk remained with the tiny embryo inside. Finally, the individual fingers wrapped it tightly and pushed it up into the palm of the metal arm like a cannon being loaded. A small, green light flickered on just above the claw—it was a hole with illuminated walls, just big enough to accept the four-inch spike of one of the devices on the shelf.

He picked one at random, inserted it into the illuminated hole on the metal arm, and gave it a quarter-turn to lock it in place. The device flashed red, emitted a quiet buzzing sound, and then rotated *itself* back in the opposite direction. Gil almost didn't react quickly enough to catch the device as it was rejected from the arm. He put it back on the base and picked a different device—one with a green light.

The arm reacted immediately. It rose up and maneuvered to one of the empty stalls on the left side of the room, flashed red, and loudly blared a deep tone.

"Oh no," Gil said. He knew they had to have heard that. The arm swung to the adjacent stall, flashed, and sounded its alarm again. "Oh no," he said again. It swung to the empty stall on the other side of the room, flashed again, and sounded its alarm just as the newcomer and Jeltz bolted into the room. "Oh no," he whined, shaking his head.

As the arm reached the carcass-occupied stall, flashed green, and then pleasantly chimed, Jeltz pushed Gil out of the way and jammed its open palm on the column's button in an attempt to interrupt whatever was happening; it didn't work. The newcomer leaped into the air, gripping the metal arm and wrapping its free hand around the device. The alien forced it to unlock and then ripped the device from the metal arm as it lowered into the mangled corpse and ejected the embryo into a mess of ground beef. The embryo had been surrounded in some sort of fluid-filled sack and, regardless of how it would have worked on a live cow, it unceremoniously slapped into the spoiling meat like a water balloon. The metal arm rose up, folded itself back into the ceiling, and disappeared. The hatch door slid shut behind it.

The newcomer inspected the device to ensure the green light remained, then walked over to the column and put it back on its base. Both of the aliens stared at Gil, who suddenly seemed to be in a trance. He stared past them, but not in his trained acting-blind gaze—his mind was racing.

Gil stepped around the newcomer and took a closer look at the dead cow. In the corner of the stall, the sixth device stood upright, still caked in Kif's week-old guts. There was no green light. He looked down at the floor and saw small, bloody footprints leading away from the corpse and into the corridor. He hadn't noticed them before; the surface of the floor was so dark that the cow's blood almost looked black against it. Now dry, they looked like no more than patches of matte finish on the otherwise glossy panels.

Looking back at the clear containers, he compared the number of cattle to the number of crewmembers aboard the ship. He finally looked back up at the newcomer, who gave Gil the slightest of affirmative nods.

"Oh, God, it *is* you, isn't it?" He wasn't sure how they went about reproduction at home, but it was now clear to Gil that the crew of this ship didn't fly here; they were *reborn* here, their consciousnesses stored on those devices for who knows how long before being injected into a host. They'd somehow gestated into full adults, emerged from the cattle—*and how the hell did they get the cattle*—and then devoured their surrogate mothers in small rations.

Gil retched, and then vomited his last meal onto the floor. He too had taken part in devouring the cattle that'd birthed these strange creatures. No wonder the two aliens worked so fiercely to remove the device form the metal arm—their genetic material and memories rested in those devices, and Gil had very nearly shot one of their kin into a heap of dead meat. Kif wouldn't have been able to come back if Korben hadn't used the device in time, and Roger could *never* come back because it died before Korben could use the device. The former was a minor setback; the latter was manslaughter. The remaining green-lit devices held more of these aliens, aliens Gil hoped never to meet. Suppose one of the green-lit devices held the consciousness of an eight-foot-tall giant?

Gil started to sob. It was just too much. Kif—he had to admit to himself it was Kif—approached him and placed a cold and clammy hand on his shoulder, but he brushed it off. He looked up at Kif, and as the pain in his side reasserted itself, he fainted.

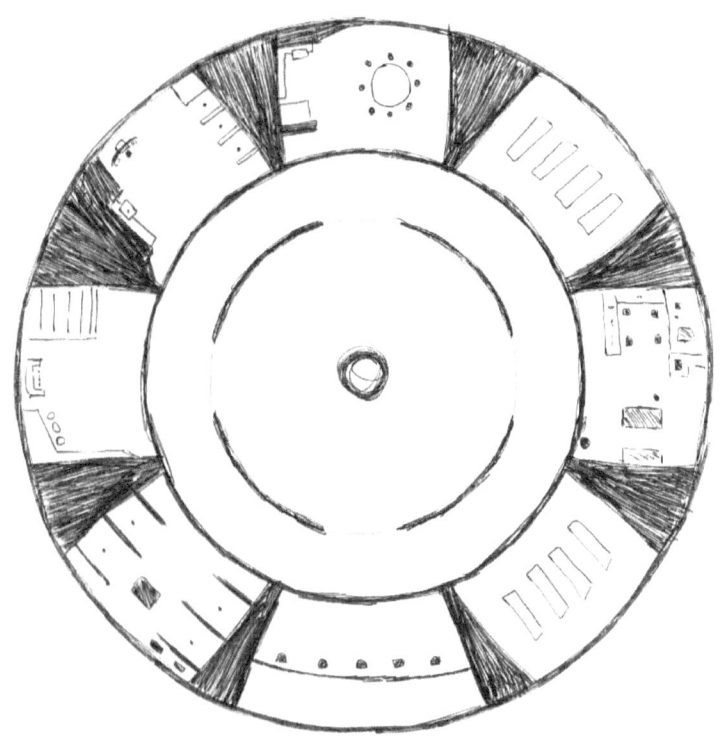

CHAPTER ELEVEN: PULLING UP STAKES

Gil awoke on his back with a start. He was surprised to once again find himself on the table of the exam room, and with his present situation flooding back to the forefront of his mind, he immediately pawed around his left side with his hand. He sat up, looked down in disbelief, and his eyes confirmed what his hand had told him: his injury had been healed. A thick and puffy pink worm of scar tissue ran the length of his wound, and though it neither looked nor felt natural, it was undeniably real.

Stroking his face, he had a feeling he hadn't been out for more than a few hours, but had no way of knowing for sure; his facial hair had outlived its usefulness as a calendar, existing now only as a greasy mess of long and scraggly hair. But as he wiped his mouth, the dried remnants of vomit told him it couldn't have been long. They had somehow completely healed his new wound in an impossibly short amount of time.

He was grateful to be rid of the searing pain, but also momentarily annoyed by this unexpected display of talent. He thought of his pincushion arm, as well as the puncture wounds the dinner plate had left in his face. There were also, of course, the various bruises dealt to his body by Korben's severed arm. He wondered resentfully why those wounds had been left to heal naturally, but as he looked around the exam room and saw Kif, he remembered the short alien had been dead for most of his stay. Jeltz was also present, working on something in the center chamber, but Gil doubted that one had anything to do with his care; he concluded it was likely Kif's expertise that led to his speedy recovery.

Gil swung his legs to the side of the table, shimmied to the edge, and got to his feet. Grimacing as he stood up, he felt the sweat-heavy weight of his clothes and remembered his soreness. Though he felt some benefits of sleeping in a warmer environment on a comparatively soft surface, the ache of a heavy workout lingered in his joints, and the vomiting had caused severe soreness in his chest—deep breaths were painfully difficult, forcing him to get by on short, shallow inhales.

He saw that a glass of water and a fresh plate of cubes lay near him. Hungry as he was, he didn't think he could bear to eat anymore of the meat now that he knew what it was. He picked up the glass and drank the water, which quenched his thirst and wet his sandpapery throat. He left the plate of food alone.

A thud came from somewhere else in the corridor, followed by the sound of two dull materials sliding against each other. Gil saw Jeltz pushing the clear containers of cattle pieces from the mystery room—no, the labor and delivery room—to the center room, where it would open the lids and tip them over, sending the contents cascading out and clattering onto the floor. The spinning disc had risen again to its eight-foot height, and at the bottom of Jeltz's growing pile of bones, Roger's grey feet could be seen sticking out. He found it odd that, given Roger had truly died, they'd still chosen to dispose of it in such an undignified manner.

The last container was the worst to watch: eyes, various organs, and gallons of fluid spilled out and flowed to the dip in the room like a moat around a boney castle. While the pieces were in different stages of decay, Gil was shocked that nothing in the foul stew seemed to be very old—he'd been on the ship for somewhere between eight and nine days, yet the cattle couldn't have been in those containers for much longer.

How does that work? he wondered. It was strange, having all but verbal confirmation that the devices could merely transfer consciousness—not duplicate it—meaning death was final. *Otherwise, Roger would have been able to come back... at least a previous version of himself. I mean... I guess I get the basic premise. They bring a large animal onboard, and then shove one of their embryos into it that's been infused with... someone else's... essence?* He stared at the short alien for a moment, who looked to be taking an inventory of the odd brain-transference devices. *Looks like Kif came back with his memories, mannerisms, and even his physical features intact. He also gestated in less than a week, which is insane, but I have to accept it. What I don't get is how the cattle got onto the ship in the first place.*

And judging by the age of the cattle parts, it looks like they popped out and then wasted no time at all picking me up. Did they lie dormant in those devices during the trip here? Are they ancient? Was that their solution for traveling long distances—digitize yourself and sleep for a thousand years? That's... incredibly inelegant and wasteful. That would mean effectively killing yourself to enter the device, being birthed when you reached your destination, killing yourself a second time to reenter the device to go back home, and then being birthed yet again when you returned. That's two physical bodies discarded per round trip, but I guess it's a workaround for interstellar travel. And then when they get here, there's the whole miracle of birth and all that, but where's the caretaker to ensure that everything comes together? Who makes sure the embryos get into the cattle? Autopilot? There has to be some system that turns itself on at some point.

Gil recalled seeing a cheesy video years ago that claimed to be footage of a cow in Argentina being sucked up into a flying saucer in broad daylight. It'd been good for a laugh at the time, and not much else, but maybe that was real too. Maybe the same ship he stood on now flew straight down in the early 1980s to pick up its target without any consideration of what time it was or who might be watching.

He was getting frustrated. There were multiple sections of the puzzle that he'd managed to piece together, but they all sat on his mental coffee table in unorganized clumps. In one completed section, he saw a picture of aliens coming back to Earth after many repeat trips in order to cure an illness they'd somehow contracted. Another section of the puzzle showed a vessel that'd traveled to Earth at speeds comparable to what modern-day astronauts could achieve. With its crew digitized and embryos frozen, the ship could have been launched hundreds or even thousands of years ago, completely powered down with no need to produce heat or provide sustenance. And once they arrived, they never left—the four of them he knew of and the three still dormant in the remaining devices could be responsible for every single abduction claim ever reported in history. He didn't know what triggered the ship to come to life when it neared Earth, but that was just another part of the puzzle.

A final chunk of the section showed two aliens who seemed experienced—knowledgeable of human anatomy and one who even had good bedside manner. Next to them stood a pompous but completely clueless alien, and towering above all of them was an aggressive hothead, convinced that Gil was a deadly threat to it, its crew, and its species. It had come down on Gil as if the human were a ruthless criminal jovially preying on the helpless.

All of these sections couldn't quite fit together yet to form a completed picture. Separately, each portion seemed true enough, but the edges of the puzzle pieces just didn't match up.

Jeltz returned to the corridor and closed all of the sliding glass windows. The clear containers had been returned to the cattle room, cleaned and neatly stacked by the column containing the dwindling supply of alien embryos. Looking back to the center chamber, Gil saw the bottom of the room descend, and then everything was gone in an instant. He hardly noticed, however, lost in thought over the implications of their strange technology.

How many animals had they attempted to use as surrogates before settling on cattle? How many of their own died after jutting from smaller animals like a sheep or a pony, half-baked but bursting from their host with no room to grow? Had a hippopotamus ever been optioned? What if it came time to vacate and they found in horror that they couldn't break through? Or what if they had, but then realized the meat, as sustenance, was inedible, or too gamey?

And then a new thought crept into Gil's mind: had a device like that ever been used on a human being? He looked at Kif again, still occupied with its cleanup. *What if he wants to jab me with one of those things? I'd wake up later, having been digitized, paired with one of their embryos, and reborn as some sort of freak.*

He asked himself if that was exactly what the not-quite-human creatures were in those most famous abduction tales, like that guy from Brazil who'd been asked to have sex with the naked, almost-but-not-quite woman aboard their ship: honest-to-goodness human beings forever trapped in a hybrid body. What if all the tales of human pregnancies being stolen aboard flying saucers were attempts to return past abductees to their former selves?

Would a hybrid appear more human, or more alien? Gil thought if he were to wake up and discover he'd been morphed into some bizarre, black-eyed creature, he wouldn't give them the chance to try and change him back; he'd make a beeline for the door in the exit chamber, slide it open, and just suck them all out into space to suffocate and die.

He was startled from his thoughts when Kif approached him from behind and lightly gripped his right wrist. Gil weakly pulled his arm away from the cool and clammy grip, and glanced distrustfully at the alien before his vision blurred. He'd been crying, lost in thought about his captors and their barbaric tech. He wiped away the tears.

He considered asking Kif what it wanted, but knew there wouldn't be much of a point. Instead, he simply raised his eyebrows questioningly. The alien gestured with its head down the corridor at the cockpit, and started walking. Gil reluctantly followed.

Jeltz had completely finished cleaning out the strange room and stood waiting in the cockpit. It stared at Kif and Gil as they approached, and to its side sat Korben in the seat closest to the two approaching. Its eyes were open, staring blankly like a movie prop at the shuttered cockpit windows.

Kif, arms holding all seven of the strange devices, made its way to the center chair and began moving its free hand over the control board. Nimble fingers danced across the surface, pressing buttons and flipping switches until a flat panel moved to the side and revealed a recessed row of ten small holes. The sight had become familiar to Gil, illuminated holes just big enough to accept the spiked end of their strange devices. Kif plugged the devices it held into the recessed panel of outlets, one by one, until all seven were out of its arms. The three green-lit devices were inserted fully and turn-locked, while the inactive four were merely set inside similar to how a pencil rests in a pencil cup. One of these inactive devices was then connected to a small cable that ran to another section of the control board.

From his peripheral vision, Gil saw Kif turn to face him. But his gaze had been locked on the back of Korben's grey head, sticking over the back of the chair like a round lump of uncooked pizza dough. He could hear his own heart beating in his chest as he looked at it, the ambient noise of the ship fading away to dull fuzz, and wondered how the featureless mound could be so menacing. He stared as one would stare at a movie screen, waiting for some popcorn-spilling jump scare to send him running. Gil wanted so badly to grab one of those devices and stab the spike through the top of that skull; to lock Korben away forever like a spirit in a ghost trap.

He looked up at Kif, who had waited patiently for his attention. With its eyes locked on Gil, Kif reached around and pushed a sliding knob. The cockpit window opened up, and Gil turned his head to the left to see out. His knees buckled, and he nearly fainted at the sight out the window. Gil knew instantly what he was looking at. It was Earth—bright, and big, and blue, and beautiful. It filled the entire length of the window—they were close. Fresh tears erupted, and Gil was confident it was finally time for him to go home.

Assured that Gil had gotten the right idea, Kif turned back to the control board. Now both of its hands worked, flipping switches and pressing buttons until Gil heard a small motor whirring from behind him. Jeltz turned around to look into the center chamber, and Gil followed suit. The metal chandelier in the center of the ship moved down, pushed by two extending poles attached to the circular structure's perimeter. Curiosity drove Gil to wander closer, into the center room and just inches away from the orange disc and its hanging counterpart. Above the chandelier, Gil saw a wide cone of round speakers which had previously been tucked away in the ceiling. After the poles had brought the chandelier down about three feet, they slowly turned the strange apparatus upside down and ascended back to the ceiling—now the cone of speakers pointed downwards, while the stalactites morphed into stalagmites and disappeared into the hull of the ship. It rose so high that even the speakers were partially recessed into the ceiling, meaning the stalagmites were now poking out of the top of the ship like a mess of antennae.

After a confusing moment, Gil brought his hands to his head and covered his ears in a panic to shield them from the abrupt and loud cacophony of noise that erupted from the speakers. A mix of radio static and what sounded like Morse code blared so loudly that Gil didn't think he'd be able to hear himself scream. He turned and ran for the cockpit. The sound faded out and then stopped completely as he reached the three aliens.

"What the hell was that?" he shouted. He looked down at the row of devices, and saw that only two of their lights remained illuminated. "What the..."

Kif pressed the single button on another of the two active devices, which triggered a second wave of ear-piercingly loud static and beeps. And then only a single light shone from the row of seven devices. As Gil recovered from this new audio assault, Kif pressed the button of the last device, triggering a third and final blast of sound. Across the entire row of devices, none of their lights remained on.

"What just happened?" Gil asked. He gestured his head towards the devices. "Your buddies just went dark. Did you—are they gone?" Of course, he received no response. Instead, Kif simply motioned him closer.

Kif guided him to the chair closest to Korben, and had him sit down.

The alien buckled him in the seat, and then took its own seat in the center chair. Jeltz buckled up in the chair to Kif's right.

Gil, safely strapped in, first looked to Kif on his right, and then to his left. Korben, not even two feet away from Gil, stared at him intensely. His eyes were locked with the alien's for a painful moment, and then he forced his gaze ahead of himself at the vision of Earth through the window. He could still feel Korben's eyes on him—an uncomfortable warmth that made him shiver.

As the ship approached Earth, all four of them began to shake wildly in their seats. The turbulence was intense. The window turned bright orange as flames licked the hull of the ship, and the heat caused beads of sweat to appear and run from Gil's forehead down to his eyes. He wished he could shield his ears from the sound—the awful thunder fell on him as though he stood at the base of a waterfall. He could hear himself screaming, so it was at least more manageable than the strange radio static from before.

In between breaths, he heard the distinct and quick sound of fabric being torn. It came from his left. He whipped his head around— Korben's stare be damned—and swore that he'd seen the giant's right arm move. Gil's eyes went wild, darting back and forth between the tall alien's hand, its eyes, the straps, and everything else to his left. He began to scream, and looked back to his right.

"I think something just happened!" he screamed desperately. "I think I heard him break his seatbelt or something! Hey!" Kif didn't turn its head to face him, possibly under the assumption that Gil was merely frightened by the turbulence. He looked forward again, terrified but unsure what he could do. If he heard right, if he really did hear Korben tearing its straps, it meant the behemoth cleverly waited for something loud enough to drown out the sound of his escape. And with Gil now strapped to his seat like someone in an electric chair, Korben could dispose of him before the others could possibly have a chance to react.

But nothing happened. They successfully reentered Earth's

atmosphere, and the ship returned to its quiet operation. They had at first flown in at such an angle as to run face first into the ground, but the ship leveled out a couple hundred feet in the air and then seemed to hover in place. It was daytime. Gil had seen them close in on California, and hoped the ship had targeted a location somewhere near his home. The last thing he saw before the ship turned upwards was a meadow. Then it was just blue skies.

Kif and Jeltz got up from their seats, and then unstrapped Gil. He got up as well, and then quickly backed up into the corridor—he couldn't wait to put some distance between Korben and himself.

"Watch out for that one," he said, pointing to Korben. "Look, I don't know exactly what happened, but I heard something—something like torn fabric. I think he tore his seatbelt off or something. He might try and come after me again."

Kif and Jeltz just stared blankly.

He pointed emphatically at Korben. "Come on, don't you get it? He's faking it—I don't think he's tied up anymore!" Gil looked optimistically at Kif, who seemed to have just had an epiphany. Kif pointed at Jeltz, and then up into the sky. Then it pointed to Korben, and again, up into the sky. It pointed at Gil, then down towards Earth, and finally pointed at itself before pointing up into the sky one last time. The optimism drained from Gil's face. "I don't... what—what are you trying to say?"

Kif turned around, grabbed one of the four devices which were not locked into the row of holes, and faced Jeltz. Jeltz, who stood behind the chairs in the clearing of the room near the corridor, looked at Gil, narrowed its eyes, and give him a single nod. A puzzled Gil shrugged and said nothing. Looking back at Kif, Jeltz took a deep breath, closed its eyes, brought its arms to its side, and put its chin up. The alien looked proudly expectant, as if preparing to receive an award.

Instead, Kif took the device and cracked the sharp end into Jeltz's forehead, pressing the single button and beginning the transfer process. Gil found this uncomfortable to watch, and it was just as jarring as Kif's transition, but he felt he had a grip on why it was being done— discarding their physical bodies to lie dormant as a collection of computer files, either to wait until the next time a visit to Earth was required, or for the long trek back home.

Gil's half-baked understanding quickly evolved, however, as Kif withdrew the device. Jeltz predictably fell over, first knocking its knees against the metal, then collapsing sideways with its head pointing into the corridor. Kif quickly wiped the guts from the green-lit device with its free hand, then plugged and locked it back into the control board. A second later, its thumb pressed the single button and triggered yet another series of static and tones. The device was now dark and inactive.

"Where'd he go?" Gil asked. And to his surprise, Kif actually answered by simply pointing a long finger up towards the ceiling. "Up?" he started, then trailed off, suddenly completing another section of his mental puzzle. Jeltz was gone—not dead, but away from the ship.

The alien had briefly been stored within the device, but now existed somewhere else—somewhere outside, broken down into kilobytes and shot out in the form of radio waves. And somewhere, something must have been set up to receive the transmission. They had both looked so comfortable with the process. Dozens, maybe even hundreds of them had used the method as an interstellar light speed highway to visit the ship, study Earth, and fly back home.

"You sent him away, didn't you?" Gil asked softly.

Kif struggled a little bit to hoist Jeltz up, but got the corpse into its arms and staggered to the exam room. It laid Jeltz on the shelf of the wide oven, slid the doors shut, and pressed some buttons that got the heat going. *Of course*, Gil thought, *they can't just spit the bodies out when we're a couple hundred feet in the air over Earth.* Flames had come to life and began to eat into the corpse, and the smell of the flesh forced Gil to run out of the room—it was unbearable. He turned back when he reached the chairs of the cockpit and saw that, despite their dulled senses, even Kif wore a slight grimace. At the entrance leading into the center room, Kif executed a number of swiping gestures on a phantom touchscreen that shut the door leading to the exam room. The stench was now greatly reduced, but Gil no longer wondered why they favored shooting their kin out into space.

The short alien grabbed another of the inactive devices and approached the restrained Korben. Gil was still nervous about what he was sure he'd heard during the reentry into Earth's atmosphere, but the feeling was dwarfed by his overwhelming relief that the tall one would finally be gone.

"Do it!" Gil demanded. "Don't waste any time, just get him out of here and be done with it."

Kif walked in front of the leftmost chair where Korben sat, and made eye contact with the tall alien. After a short period of silence, Kif offered one of its familiar nods and lifted the device. The suspense was killing Gil, who tried to be patient and failed.

"Just do it, goddammit!" he spat, and then started towards Kif as if to guide the device to Korben's forehead. Kif finally swung its arm down, but a large and strong hand suddenly rose up and gripped the short alien's forearm. Gil let out a high-pitched, "No!" as Korben used its left hand—fully formed at last—to wrestle the device free, flip it around, and drive the tip harshly into the right side of Kif's skull. For the second time since Gil came aboard, Kif convulsed and shed its physical body, falling limply on top of the seated Korben. The giant ripped the device out, pushed the corpse off of itself, and as the body slapped against the floor, Korben worked to release its various straps.

With a dozen straps and buckles now dangling from its seat, Korben rose up, anchored the device, and sent Kif away into space. Now, only it and Gil remained—nothing would stand in Korben's way.

It whirled around triumphantly, ready to choke the life out of the human, but its furious eyes quickly reshaped into an expression of shock; Gil was nowhere in sight.

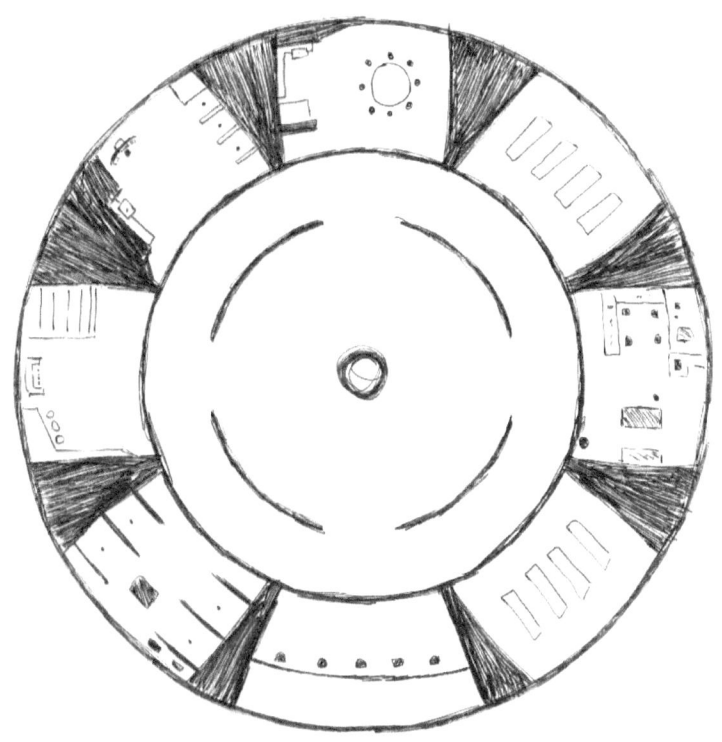

Chapter Twelve: Pursuit

Not a chance, Gil thought. *I might just be a couple hundred feet from my front door. I'm not going down now.* As soon as Korben had shaken off its various seatbelts and started to stand up, Gil quickly bolted left and power-walked down the corridor while Korben was still preoccupied with the control board. He knew Korben would be coming for him soon, so he had to think fast if he wanted to have any chance of survival.

As he reached the exam room, he covered his ears and winced in pain as the sound of Kif's exit rang through the ship. Spinning around to look behind him, he wished he had walked the other way through the corridor—he recalled that a couple of the glass spears stood in the exit room, whereas Kif had closed the exam room to mask the stench of Jeltz's burning flesh. A slew of knives and makeshift prison shanks waited behind the planked door, but Gil knew he didn't have enough time to try and get it open.

Now, with the exit room on the opposite side of the ship and all but one of the doors to the center room closed, Gil had to make a half-circle through the corridor—past the beds, past the kitchen, and past the bathroom before he could finally reach something he could wield as a weapon. He hoped Korben had chosen to follow Gil in the same direction; otherwise, he'd run into the giant en route and it would all be over.

He broke into a run, but stopped suddenly as he became aware of two things happening simultaneously. To his left, he noticed that all of the center room doors were opening. There were only four of them, but the openings would give anyone in the center of the ship a clear indication of Gil's movement. To his right, Gil saw that all of the outer chambers' planked doors were sliding shut. His heart sank. He knew he wouldn't have enough time to massage one of the doors open again, so without any time at all to think, Gil ducked into the kitchen and tried to look for some sort of hiding place.

"Oh no!" he shouted, almost involuntarily as he realized what he'd done. As soon as he entered the kitchen, the room sensed his presence and the planked doors retreated in the opposite direction. Korben had initiated some simple commands via a phantom touchpad that would simply close all of the chambers, and as a result was able to instantly narrow down Gil's location to the only room that remained open. Gil watched hopelessly as all of the other rooms he could see disappeared behind dozens of planks.

"Okay, think," he coached himself. His eyes darted around the room. "There's got to be a knife in here somewhere." *How else could they cut up all that meat?* He scanned the room and started to panic—a water dispenser, a refrigerator, an inset shelf with snugly-secured plates and glasses, some sort of a dish washer, and a table surrounded by eight stumpy seats was all that Gil could see in the room. Not a single cabinet or drawer in sight that might contain something sharp.

He moaned in frustration. He could already hear Korben's heavy footfalls, picking up speed as Gil's location was narrowed down to the kitchen. With a sudden burst of inspiration, a thin plan formed in Gil's head. He grabbed a short stack of plates and ran for the exit.

Gil reached the threshold at the edge of the kitchen and stepped into the corridor when Korben came upon him. The giant sent a balled up fist directly into the side of Gil's face, nearly knocking him over and forcing him to drop his armful of dishes. The plates clattered to the floor, some of them shattering upon impact and settling in tiny, jagged splinters. Gil staggered to the kitchen table before dizzyingly falling backwards against one of its stumpy seats. As if swinging at a swarm of insects, the disoriented man blindly flailed his fists and hoped his senses would return to him. Korben stepped in front of him and delivered a powerful, open-handed slap with its right hand against Gil's face. He shouted in response to the stinging pain, and then unskillfully punched Korben around the torso several times before receiving another blow to the head.

Gil, who had never been a particularly adept fighter, knew that he couldn't win a fistfight with an angry, seven-foot-tall alien—in fact, he didn't think he could survive many more of the intense punches. His only hope was his shaky plan, and it required him to put enough distance between himself and Korben to grab a few of the unbroken plates and run into the center room.

Tucking his legs underneath himself, Gil put both his hands on Korben's belly and kicked off from the right-angled point where the floor rose into a seat. The surprised alien fell over backwards, landing in the shattered material of the plates and barking in pain.

Gil looked around and saw that five of the plates remained intact. The others either sat in splinters or shards not big enough to bother picking up. On his knees, he gathered up the plates and struggled to get to his feet. Just as he began to run, one of Korben's long legs swept Gil's own out from under himself, causing him to lose his balance, spin around, and fall flat on his back. The plates dropped out of his arms again, and two of them broke into smaller pieces. Only three plates remained.

He struggled again to get to his feet, but Korben quickly stood up and pressed one of its feet against Gil's chest to force him back down. It folded the same leg at the knee and set its weight on Gil's ribcage, who tried and failed several times to take a swing at Korben. It wrapped its new left hand around Gil's neck, once again choking him with what felt like a rubber-coated vice grip, and then used its right hand to deliver two hard punches to Gil's face.

Gil tried to cough, but couldn't. Blood swelled from his nose and mouth as he desperately tried for a gulp of air. His fingers reached for Korben's face, but the thing's arms were longer than his—it was no use. Gil was blacking out. He worried it was all over, and it would have been if Korben's arrogance—it hadn't expected much resistance from the human—hadn't convinced the alien to move its face closer to watch the man die.

With the alien's face now in reach, Gil took both hands and drove his unkempt fingernails into Korben's eyes. Korben roared, the heavy and thick eyelids snapping shut and forcing Gil's hands away from the slimy orbs. It rolled over off of Gil, gripping its face and moaning in pain.

There was no time to lose. Gil gathered up the three plates and forced himself to his feet one last time—he could feel exhaustion coming on again, and if he were knocked down just one more time, he knew he wouldn't be able to get back up. He ran straight for the center room, past the orange disc, then stopped abruptly and whirled back around as soon he reached the corridor outside the cockpit. He stared almost clear across the ship into the kitchen, and waited for Korben to rise up and come after him.

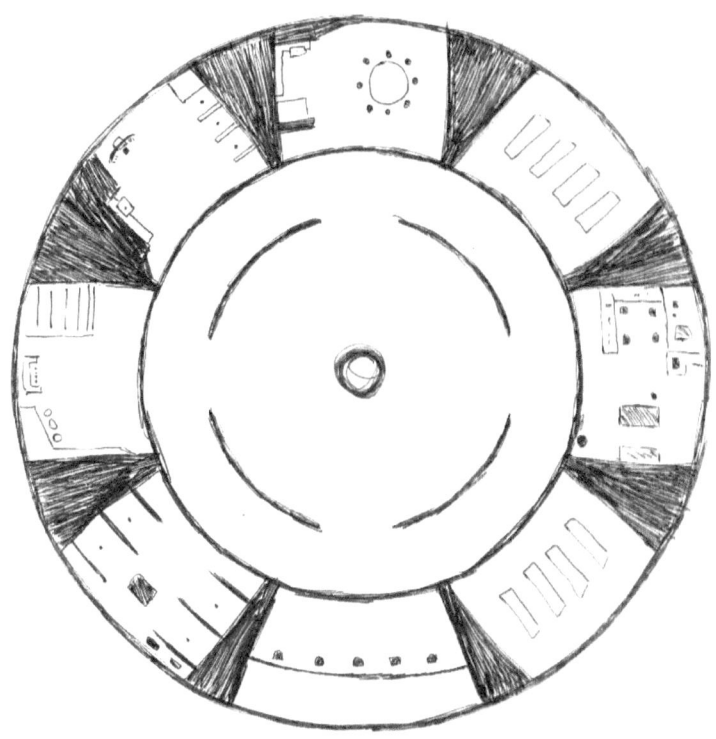

Chapter Thirteen: Casting Spells

Korben opened its eyes, shook its head, and got to its feet. It was furious, and beyond ready for the ordeal to be over. Blinking away the last remnants of pain, it stared across the ship, spotted Gil, and broke into a sprint immediately—out of the kitchen, past the corridor, and into the center room. Just before it reached the spinning disc, it finally saw the blaze in Gil's eyes as the human lifted the three plates he held above his head, and then chucked them all at once at the spinning orange disc.

As soon as the plates left his hands, Gil raced into the corridor and pressed his back against the inner wall. He didn't know what to expect exactly, but hoped the plates would shatter as they had when Korben broke one over his face, and that the disc was spinning fast enough to distribute the mess.

It turned out to be more powerful than he had expected. The

dishes hit the disc and exploded like a light bulb dropped into the blades of an industrial fan, sending little shards of glass-like material all throughout the center room. A small amount even blew into the corridor and near Gil's feet. He heard a shriek, the sprinkling of tiny splinters, and finally a loud thud. He stood for a moment, shaking, holding his breath, wet with his own sweat and blood. At last, he moved to the opening and peered his head around the edge of the doorway, where he saw Korben, face down on the ground. He knew the alien couldn't be dead, but hoped it was at least unconscious.

Gil considered going to the exit chamber, grabbing one of the clear spears, and then doing away with Korben for good—right through the eye, just like Roger. Or perhaps he could go into the cockpit, grab one of those devices, and simply send the alien away. Either solution would have allowed Gil to take his time getting away from the ship, and he liked both of those approaches... but the alien still terrified him.

I don't want to get close enough for him to grab me. I guess I could throw the spear at him, but what if I miss? Suppose it hit the floor and he wakes up? Or that I only wound him and he wakes up angrier than ever? If we were still in space, then I might have been able to figure out a way to close all the doors and open the hatch in the middle—that would have been a rude awakening—but that's not possible now.

Ultimately, doubt kept Gil from taking further action against Korben. After a painstaking moment of indecision, Gil decided the alien could wake up later—hopefully after Gil was already gone—and then just go back to wherever it came from. He got himself moving again towards the cockpit.

Gil moved quickly. He wiped the drying blood from his face and brought his filthy hand to the center plank of the cockpit. He prepared himself to rub the plank to temperature and open the room, but the lightest touch seemed to activate the touch screen. He looked at his hand and wondered, *is it not heat-sensitive? Is it something in my blood?* But as the planks silently slid open and he saw the control board, the touch technology no longer interested him.

How the hell am I going to get out of here? he thought, looking over the wide control bay. It was no more familiar to him now than the first time he saw it. He knew one of the buttons controlled the window, and that one of the buttons controlled the gravity; the rest was still mostly a mystery. Starting from the left side of the chamber and working his way to the right, he carefully stepped around Kif's second corpse and examined the controls.

Okay, Kif piloted the ship to Earth and changed our orientation a couple of times, which means the flight stick is probably the key. Gil used his index finger to lightly push the flight stick forward, and the flying saucer responded instantly, moving forward with enough force that Gil felt it. He wrapped his hand around the stick and pulled back to stop the ship, but over corrected; the spacecraft shot in the opposite direction, the sudden change causing Gil to fall forward onto the control deck and push the flight stick forward.

"Shit!" Gil shouted as the spacecraft shot forward again, flinging him harshly but safely into the center chair of the cockpit. With his hand still wrapped around the stick, he gently pulled back until it stood straight up and the ship finally came to a standstill. He let out a loud sigh of relief. He released the flight stick in frustration and asked aloud, "How do I bring this thing down?"

He craned his neck around to make sure Korben was still unconscious behind him, and then examined the various buttons and switches that covered the flight stick more closely. After some trial and error, he located a small, spring-loaded switch on the side of the stick that he could pull back, but reverted to its normal position when he released it. With the switch fully extended, he *very* gently pushed forward on the flight stick. A slight sensation of weightlessness rose in him, and he smiled. "Bingo."

Because only blue skies were visible outside the window, Gil initially had no idea how quickly he was descending. It could have been just a few feet per minute, or something closer to a freefall. Slowly, foothills came into view in the distance, and then trees. Gil pulled back a bit on the flight stick to slow his descent, and after a few more moments, the ship came to a harsh and immediate stop as it bumped into the ground. Gil grunted loudly, the force knocking the wind out of him, and then rested his head on the back of the chair. Panting, but overjoyed that he was on the ground, he looked down at the corpse and mumbled, "I'm not exactly a leaf on the wind, am I?"

Then Gil got up from the chair and headed for the exit chamber.

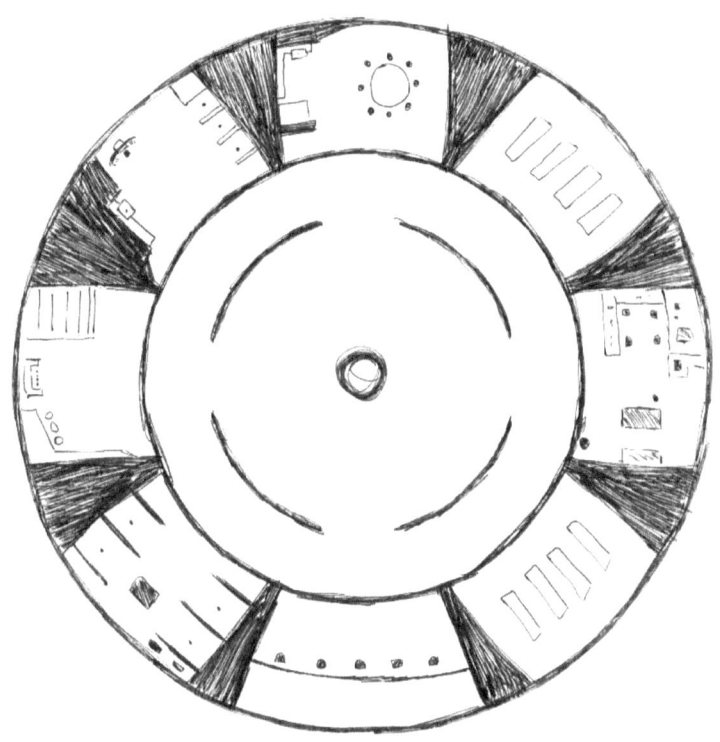

Chapter Fourteen: Trapped

Gil looked up at the sliding hatch at the top of the small staircase in the exit chamber. He'd checked on Korben when he turned around in the cockpit, and again when he reached the opening behind him. Though Korben's body had certainly moved since Gil's improvised bomb went off, he attributed that to the motion of the ship. The alien was breathing, but was situated in such an uncomfortable position that Gil still figured Korben hadn't yet come to.

Now, the door to the outside world was finally in front of him, and for the first time since his abduction, he thought of his home. He longed to settle into his couch—to lay in his bed and use his shower. He longed to grill up a real meal and enjoy a cold beer in any of the various glasses he'd procured from defunct bars.

But as he set his foot on the first step, he hesitated. He put both feet back on the floor and turned around.

Focusing his eyes on Korben again, Gil stared for nearly a full minute. When he felt confident the alien was absolutely unconscious, he walked forward until he was back in the corridor and the exit chamber silently slid shut behind him. With his eyes trained on Korben's body, he quickly and quietly sidestepped to his left until he reached the area outside the kitchen. There was no view into the center room between the two areas, so Gil held his breath until he made it to the kitchen and could see the tall alien's body again.

He spun around and used his bloody hand to enter the chamber, and once inside, retrieved two of the odd drinking glasses. He had to force them out of the snug containers which surely kept them from shattering against the wall each time the ship moved. The detour was reckless—or, really, stupid—but he couldn't help it. What better example of a failed startup could there possibly be than this? How could he resist nabbing two of the strange cups to add to his eclectic collection at home?

But when he had the cups in hand, Gil pivoted on his heel and had to bite back a scream. *He was just here*, he thought. *Had to be less than a minute!*

The spot where Korben lay just a moment before was now empty, occupied only by shards of glass and a smear of green-grey blood. There were no bloody footsteps to indicate a path, but the creatures weren't exactly brimming with blood. Gil listened hard for footsteps, but the only sound in the entire ship was the hum of the spinning disc. He didn't smell anything either. Only the planked walls obscuring the ship's chambers could be seen from side to side, but dead ahead, Gil saw the tall chair in the center of the open cockpit.

He whirled around, pressed his back against the inner wall of the corridor, and clung to the edge of the open doorway. In front of him, the kitchen's walls silently slid shut. He could now see the cockpit again through the reflection of the kitchen's porthole. *Why didn't I just leave?* he wondered. *Why did I need these stupid cups?* From the reflection, Gil saw a weary Korben stagger into view in the distance. The alien was in the cockpit on the opposite end of the ship with one huge hand resting against the tall chair for balance. Gil involuntarily held his breath when Korben stopped and glanced into the center room, hoping it hadn't seen the kitchen's planked doors close. *Okay, Gil,* he coached himself, *he's gotta be at least forty feet away from you. He looks hurt bad, so if you keep some distance between the two of you, you can quickly get to the exit chamber, activate the door, open the hatch, and hop out. Then you'll be gone before he can get to you. You can do this. You can do this.*

Gil had a feeling Korben might search the ship to look for him, but the alien had apparently made up its mind that Gil had already escaped. Korben sauntered around to the front of the chair and sat down. Gil tucked the two glasses into the crook of his arm, and tip toed the twenty feet to the space outside the exit chamber. He held his breath again, and the ship was so quiet that he literally heard pins drop—it was Korben, sitting in the tall chair, plucking the shards from his punctured body and dropping them onto the floor.

Gil wiped his face, lunged forward, and used his bloody hand to get the door open. He ran forward as the planks spread apart and grabbed one of the clear spears without waiting to see whether or not Korben noticed. As he ascended the small staircase and gripped the handle of the sliding door, he began to hear footsteps—first slow and far away, then heavy, fast, and loud.

Gil pulled the handle to the right, and was simultaneously pleased the door was not locked or secured in any way, and horrified that he could hardly make it budge. The damn thing was heavy. He immediately flew into a panic, loudly jerking the door with reckless abandon—there was no point in sneaking around now. When a thin beam of sunlight finally penetrated the crack he'd worked open, he poked the spear out and used it as a lever to force a foot of space. The warm sunlight fell on his face and he burst into tears. He quickly grabbed the cups with the fingers of his right hand and chucked them out through the opening, hoping they'd land on something soft. He finally used both hands to force the levered door open, propped the spear in the door jam, and ran up the stairs as the footsteps behind him broke into a sprint.

CHAPTER FIFTEEN: THE WAYPOINT

Free at last, Gil tripped as he eagerly ran through the hatch and then clumsily rolled down the edge of the flying saucer. As he reached the edge and fell into the long grass, he heard the door loudly slide back on its rollers, followed by a desperate shriek from Korben. But the door did not close. On his back, Gil caught the spear as it rolled down. *I must have accidentally kicked it with my foot.* He pointed the spear upwards and readied himself to surprise Korben when the alien would inevitably come over the edge. He was breathing hard, hands shaking, and pissing all over himself.

Korben was loud. It angrily shouted and banged around the top of the ship, but Gil couldn't see it. The edge of the spacecraft extended several feet beyond the walls of its eight rooms, tapering off and ending with a waist-high vertical drop. It was here that Gil waited, grew impatient, and then finally got up to see why Korben refused to come after him.

Gil sighed with relief when he got to his feet and saw the alien. The shattered plates resulted in many pockmarks on Korben's skin—some shards remained embedded and stuck out like tiny spikes, while others had fallen out and left behind oozing holes. It had lunged through the door just as Gil inadvertently kicked his makeshift lever out of place, causing the heavy door to slam shut on Korben. The door dug into the small of Korben's back, pinning its waist and sandwiching its left wrist in the opening. Although Korben was certainly strong enough to open the door with ease—it would likely remain open if pushed all the way—the alien was pinched at such an awkward angle that the haggard alien simply couldn't push the door hard enough with its right hand. Instead, it moaned and vainly reached for Gil like a zombie.

"Well, you're in a pickle, aren't you?" Gil asked, panting and resting the spear over his shoulder. "I see you're not having a whole lotta good luck with that left arm." He could feel the warm sun on his back, and the earthy scent of grass and mud was everywhere. The droning sound of the ship's spinning disc had been replaced with the drone of birds and crickets throughout the meadow, and he savored the feeling of the cool breeze and soft earth under his feet. He'd gotten a second wind, an energy he hadn't possessed before that emboldened him. "Look, I'm going to get out of here, okay? I'm sure you'll figure something out—you'll get out of this jam eventually, and then you can just fly away. Then you can stick yourself with one of those things you have in there and wake up back at home with a brand-new body." He punctuated the last sentenced with a wry smile.

Korben's attempts became more violent. It raged against the door, trying to wriggle it open, but failed. After a moment, Gil shook his head with a mix of pity and disgust.

"What do you have against me, huh? What do—what do you—hey!" Gil shouted at the alien, who continued to try and push the door open. The hard edges had begun to cut shallowly into Korben's thick skin, and its efforts were growing feebler by the second. Gil picked up a small stone and threw it as hard as he could at Korben's head. "I'm talking to you!"

The stone startled Korben, who gradually ceased struggling and turned its attention to Gil. It breathed hard through its nose and stared at the human more intensely than ever before. Gil waited for a moment, and then continued.

"None of your other buddies wanted to kill me. I think you're all a bunch of monsters, but they were downright pleasant compared to you."

Korben continued to stare at Gil.

"So what's your deal?"

Korben continued to stare at Gil, who whacked the spear against the hull of the ship.

"Stop staring at me! I know you're not deaf. You pretend like you are, but I've caught you by surprise a couple times and startled you. You *can* hear me. I think sometimes you even know what I'm saying. Maybe not exactly, but you got the drift."

Korben continued to stare at Gil.

"Okay, you're just gonna stare, huh? Is that all you want to do? Fine." Gil leaned over the hard edge of the ship and mockingly stared back at Korben, still unnerved by the detail but not as afraid as before. Korben leaned closer once the two of them made eye contact, as if participating in some sort of staring contest. Gil jumped slightly a moment later, when Korben slammed its free fist in apparent frustration against the hull of the ship. "What are—I... I don't know what you're trying to do."

Korben slammed its fist down again and stretched its neck out, getting as close to Gil as possible. Gil apprehensively stared back at the alien with confusion. He couldn't put it into words at the time, but he would later reflect that the alien looked to be constipated. Korben's head began to shake, and Gil saw its jaw muscles bulge—a clear indication that it was fiercely clenching its teeth. And before long, Gil could hear a strained, high-pitched growl escaping its thin lips. Whatever it was trying to do, it was giving it everything it had.

Gil's expression grew into sheer bewilderment. "What the hell's the matter with you?" he asked, then dropped his spear, fell to his knees, and closed his eyes.

Dark clouds hung over a rocky landscape, obscuring a strange planet's star and washing the surface in a dim light. A shallow creek flowed between two halves of a large settlement consisting of dome-shaped buildings of various sizes. Their material was black and shiny, like polished hematite, and bright artificial light spilled out of all their many openings.

Hundreds of Greys wearing black cloaks filed across a small bridge over the creek to a large dome building where many others were congregating. It was an important day. Nearly a thousand years prior, three experimental, unmanned crafts were launched into space in different directions. Though capable of impressive speeds by almost any other standards, they moved at a crawl through the vast emptiness of space. Further, the crafts weren't designed to support life for extended periods of time, and so traveled through space as lifeless hunks of material.

They were meant as waypoints—probes into the far reaches of space to search for signs of interstellar life which spacefarers could later travel to. At the time, only one method of light-speed travel had been theorized and, while highly controversial, was the only method the spacecraft could realistically be outfitted with.

Using principals of mammalian reproduction, an individual's consciousness could be scanned, digitized, paired with a young embryo within an artificial membrane, and finally injected into a large mammal for gestation. This method had proved viable hundreds of years before, when it was banned on moral grounds. Countless Greys had been paired with the embryos of non-Grey species, resulting in irreversible abominations that led to the condemnation of the technology. Its development came to be thought of as a dark period of the Greys' history.

The three spacecrafts, each powered by a highly unstable element, were only the first step in what was once considered a promising

128

program. The dominant thought of the time was that the technology of the ships would be outpaced in a manner of decades—that before the ships ever had a chance to reach anything, the Greys would devise better ships that allowed near light-speed travel with inhabitants on board. If nothing else, the hope for the three crafts was that future generations would continue to develop a viable means of light-speed travel to visit it in a more practical manner. But this was not the case. After hundreds of years with no findings from any of the three crafts, interest in the program died. Dozens of generations came and went before Earth was discovered—young and old alike were only taught about the spacecrafts for their historical context.

When a craft finally did send a transmission, the excitement belonged to a new era—an era with little interest in space travel. With the exploration program long since abandoned, the process of analyzing the data was akin to finding an ancient civilization buried under the rubble of time. For many years, the task of understanding the antique ships, the data the ships sent back, and the barbaric method of reaching a ship fell on Grey archaeologists. It was only natural, then, that many of the first travelers to Earth were not students of science, but history.

Images and data returned from the craft revealed a more colorful world with beings similar in many ways to themselves. The planet was closer to its star and thus warmer. Its bipedal inhabitants varied greatly in appearance. It was determined that contact would be beneficial for both civilizations, but without any practical means to reach the ship, the ancient and long-unused technology of consciousness transference had to be revisited. The process of understanding this long-forgotten tech took many years, and was initially met with disgust. If the ships had been launched just a couple hundred years later, they could have held lifelike robots which could be remotely controlled from home. Instead, a roundtrip for just one individual required the creation and destruction of two physical bodies.

Research concluded that an individual would have the spiked end of a stout device shoved through the skull, which would initiate a brain scan and record genetic information. The body would die in the process. The corpse would be discarded, and the digital information from the device could then be sent light years away and injected into a sack paired with a rare and precious Grey embryo—the revelation that nearly a hundred frozen embryos sat aboard each of the three ships was met with further disgust at the wastefulness of past generations.

Finally, the sack could be implanted into any large mammal, which would eventually gestate into the same Grey that had originally taken the device's sharp spike. The first member of a group to be received by the ship would trigger a primitive autopilot, which would fly to Earth to seek out any mammal large enough to accommodate their bodies. The first mammal selected ended up being the default option for all future missions—the creature was small enough to fit through the bottom hatch of the ship, but large enough to accommodate even the tallest individuals. Further, the abundant meat not consumed during gestation would provide adequate sustenance for the crew during the trip.

Those who had gone through with the procedure claimed the transition was sudden and instantaneous. They would feel the intense and traumatic pain of the spike penetrating their skulls before flailing wildly in the dark tangle of flesh and blood that separated them from the outside world. They would claw and bite their way out. The umbilical cords would be removed, and due to the nature of their restorative physiology, the hole in the belly of the new body would heal and leave nothing behind.

Using high-powered transmitters and receivers, the consciousness of a being would be sent wirelessly to the ship at faster-than-light speeds. Thus, what seemed like the blink of an eye to the traveler was actually a period of four years. After a community of hopeful travelers had risen up, the waypoint was used as a timeshare, as trips were staggered by a period of months; four months after the first group departed, another group would queue up and depart. Four months later, another group would depart, and so on.

On this important day, a little over eight years later, the first travelers to Earth's waypoint were back at home and due to emerge from the sleeping giants that grew them. A week prior, the travelers were received and downloaded, and then the entire settlement was scanned for anyone willing to donate an embryo. The scientists returned to the large dome with ten embryos—any remaining would be frozen for later use. Hundreds gathered around to inquire about the strange new world.

A large, three-legged animal covered with dense brown fur lay comatose, and then began to shake. Several individuals rushed to it with sharp blades, ready to help the returning traveler through the thick wall of flesh and bone. Once emerged, the traveler gasped for air and ripped the umbilical cord from its abdomen, then lay panting on the ground. After washing the blood from its skin and donning a robe, the traveler told of its experience.

The old spacecraft was even more archaic than expected. After emerging from the strange mammal and spilling out into the ancient ship, the traveler had clumsily guided it back to the new world and painstakingly acquired three additional animals of similar description for its digital companions. And a week later, they were all in the flesh, ready for their reconnaissance. They found no garments aboard the craft, and thus remained naked.

Initial findings were promising. The atmosphere was breathable, the water drinkable, and the beasts edible. And unlike the Greys' world, Earth spun on an axis as it rotated its star. This made most of its surface area habitable—as opposed to their own planet with its locked orbit—and as a result, the population size was astronomical. With one side of the Grey home world shrouded in permanent darkness and freezing cold, and the other scorched by the constant heat of the star, the Greys straddled the two environments along the permanent dusk of the prime meridian.

The Greys' counterpart, Earthlings, proved troublesome. They could not speak—that is, their voice could not leave the confines of their minds. Instead, their voices were audible, communicated via their vocal folds in bits and pieces using a defined series of noises. Though facial expressions seemed to be universal, since they were usually consistent with their actions, nearly all of their communication was based on sound alone. Cursory tests confirmed the suspicion that their physiology would never allow them to speak in another manner, and their capacity to accept speech from the Greys was so limited that speaking to them directly was both exhausting and potentially dangerous. So the group had to endure endless, audible babbling from the multiple Earthlings they'd brought aboard the ship. The Earthlings proved to be aggressive and hostile, but also quite weak and easy to subdue. Their anatomy was remarkably similar on the outside, but unexpectedly different on the inside. Further, like so many other animals, their species consisted of two types.

The traveler went on to explain that, though three of them had embarked on the interstellar journey, four souls had come back—in the interest of achieving some form of communication, one of the Earthlings brought aboard the ship had its consciousness digitized for the purpose of mixing the two species. The file had been embedded into a Grey embryo, in the hopes that the hybrid would be endowed with the ability to speak. With the consciousness drained from the body, a thorough autopsy had been performed, and it was discovered that the creatures were mammals. Their bodies were like plump citrus fruits, full of liquids and nearly as fragile. The travelers were commended for their efforts.

When the Earthling finally emerged from the animal and immediately set to screaming, the traveler assured everyone it was normal—all of the Earthlings had responded the same way, barking like animals and flailing about for most of the various encounters. The Earthling bellowed and writhed on the ground in its bloody mess. It was beige. Its eyes were large and colorful, and thin hairs clung to its wet body—this mix of both Grey and Earthling hardly resembled either species. When approached, it scurried to the corner like some wild thing and continued to scream itself hoarse. The Greys found the hybrid could in fact speak now, but not in any discernible way. Being close to the hybrid filled one's mind with random and broken imagery—akin to being near a rabid animal, scared and confused, trapped in a cage. Those in attendance initially looked on in confusion and wonder, but this quickly turned to annoyance, and then disdain. By the time the other travelers emerged, the hybrid had to be taken outside and kept separate from the populace.

As time went on, more groups returned with new findings. Each departing group would fill the waypoint with notes, which grew into a sizable compendium of Earthling knowledge. Various experiments were carried out. Casualties occurred only once, but the incident resulted in the loss of a physical body and, likely, the discovery of their presence. On several occasions, travelers would pair themselves with Earthling embryos to emerge as creatures somewhere in between. They would lose the ability to speak in the process, but could still engage in written communication. These new hybrids gained a cursory understanding of communication through sound. Understanding was simple enough, but moving one's mouth to form words proved difficult and time consuming. The first word many of them learned was based on its context and the frequency in which Earthlings would scream it at them: "No."

Periodically, returning crews would bring back their own hybrids, but this practice quickly became tiring—after the fourth crew returned with yet another hybrid, the practice was banned. However, due to the nature of their staggered trips, over a dozen groups would still return with hybrids without ever getting the message. This resulted in the practice of examining the consciousness files before embedding. If an Earthling consciousness could be identified, it would simply be deleted. If not, it would be birthed and then quickly sent to the outskirts with the other Earthling hybrids.

The growing hybrid colony, which had long since ceased its mindless barrage of broken imagery, was contained at the edge of the settlement—no one had any idea what to do with them. The area was avoided. Those who ventured too close often fell unconscious, their heads filled with the overwhelming but indiscernible voice of the group. It was described as the voice one hears around young children—those too young to control their voices, sending them out in every direction imaginable. They were useless, and attempts at meaningful communication were fruitless.

Returning Greys who'd spliced themselves with Earthlings were assembled into a small team and tasked with observing the hybrid Earthlings, which returned limited results. Through decades of observation and interaction, all the Greys could establish was that the hybrids wanted to rid themselves of their altered bodies and return home. They were messy, picky eaters, withdrawn and suicidal.

It was eventually decided that the hybrids must be returned home—the Greys had to make their presence known, but things would have to be made right before official contact could be established on Earth. A return trip was made with the original hybrid in tow. Through several transference attempts using freshly-extracted Earthling embryos, the visitor returned to something near normalcy before mysteriously dying. And when the crew returned, dejected and defeated, they found their appearance had somehow changed: they were bright white. This lone symptom led to fever, followed by incurable dehydration and eventual death.

The sickness spread throughout the settlement, infecting most in a matter of days. In a matter of weeks, death within the colony was a daily occurrence. Mass graves were prepared, and before long, huge swaths of the deceased were pushed towards and dropped into it. Almost all of the hybrids caught the infection, and a small number of them succumbed, but most suffered only a short fever and then fully recovered. The fact that Earthlings were able to fight the infection led to the discovery that the infection originated on Earth. And this discovery led to the conclusion that Earth had attacked—attacked in retaliation to the Greys' failed experiments, and out of fear of the unknown.

The exploration program was immediately abandoned. Four years' worth of expeditions were still due to return; however, the returns ceased after just one year, and those who did return would find themselves infected. The existing hybrids, regardless of where they originated, were summarily executed and added to one of the mass graves. Meanwhile, the Greys continued to die out, and a powerful hatred for Earth developed. Those who had opposed the program from the beginning continued to condemn it even on their deathbeds. The Earthlings were cowards, all of them—these creatures who chose to viciously attack the Greys from the shadows, and all over a misunderstanding.

Experimentation revealed that consciousness digitization could allow an individual to have the infection manually written out of its genetic code; however, without the infrastructure in place for mass-digitization and rebirth, new bodies would gestate fully recovered, only to be re-infected shortly after birth. Those who were lucky enough to form their own embryo would use it at the last possible moment for a chance at life. Others would do the same, often acquiring an embryo after violently stealing it from someone else.

Entirely too late, many began to wonder how most of the hybrids managed to fight the infection. While medical treatment administered to the Greys proved entirely unsuccessful, all but a few hybrids beat the infection without any intervention at all. Eventually, and without a single hybrid left in the colony, it was determined that the cure lay within the Earthlings' own flesh and blood.

With tens of thousands of Greys dead and buried, and with the scientific community dwindling to almost nothing, four volunteers were sought to visit Earth one last time to devise a cure. Afterwards, the ship would be set on a slow course back home, and Earth would never be visited again. In the most remote area of the settlement, four young, uninfected individuals stepped up to take the journey. The team consisted of two students of Earth anatomy, one student of history, and a first-year member of the military.

Nearly all of the remaining infected population chose to undergo long-term digitization, and then discarded their physical bodies. They would be reborn after the last travelers returned with a cure. The few Greys not already infected spread out farther and settled in neighboring areas. It was agreed that, if any embryos were to form, they would be frozen and set aside for the eventual return of the population. The team was infected before even having a chance to leave.

When the first of them awoke on the ship, it acquired four more animals from Earth's surface as quickly as possible to start the gestation process. Until the process had completed, it would spend its days cleaning out the various dead bodies that littered the ship. And when its travel companions emerged, they made themselves familiar with the technology, and then departed for the Earth.

Gil gripped the sides of his head and groaned in agony. So much information—too many concepts, too much imagery—had raced through his mind like a bullet from a gun. The blast caused him to curl over and bear down so his mind could process it all. When it finally sunk in, he allowed himself to fall over. There had been several instances over the course of Gil's abduction where, in hindsight, they must have been attempting to communicate with him. But Gil never felt anything more than anxiety. This time, though, a connection had been established and Gil saw everything in those black eyes. And judging by how taxing it seemed to have been for the exhausted alien, communicating with Gil had been no small feat. But it was essential—with the tables turned, and Korben stuck between a door and a hard place with its life in the human's hands, it had to explain itself. They both lay there panting for several minutes, Korben's thick veins pulsating heavily in its face and gradually subsiding. Then Gil finally sat up, got to his feet, and addressed the alien.

"I knew it," he proclaimed. "I got the—I had you pegged, man." He rested the spear over his shoulder again and pointed his filthy finger at the alien, turning his lips inward and shaking his head. "Look around you, man. Do you see anybody else?"

Korben followed his finger for only a moment as it darted to either direction, then stared back at Gil.

"You're just an urban legend... but you—you stole people? You turned them into some kind of freaks and then—and then killed them? You're just... you're monsters. I'm sorry about what happened to you... to your people, but you're crazy if you thought for even a second that I'd take pity on you. You gotta understand that any number of things your people were doing could have caused you to get sick. You could've caught the common cold from any of the hundreds of abductees. You could've caught some virus passed by all that cattle. Hell, if I understand all this correctly, you could've caught something from one of the pregnancies your people stole. We'll just never know, but no one knew about you guys. Not for sure anyways."

Korben continued to stare at Gil, who finally threw up his hands and asked, "You really don't have any idea what I'm saying, do you? All those missions, all those studies back at home, and still just nothing?" He didn't wait to see if Korben's stare would persist; instead, he knelt down to pick up his drinking glasses, then turned around and walked away. Once he had about ten yards of distance between them, he spun around again to look at Korben. Sticking out of the side of the ship like Korben did, Gil thought it all looked like an oversized novelty antenna ball.

Gil had the advantage. He could easily kill Korben now, drag its corpse into public view, and let the entire world see the monster. Then people could come and look at this ship, and make a big spectacle of it... but maybe that wasn't such a good idea. The most memorable moment of that forced scene was their decision to leave Earth and never come back. After all, their trips to Earth had resulted in the death of the majority of their species. They were done here. But if Gil prevented Korben from leaving—if he kept their ship from heading back home, would they send reinforcements?

Best not to risk it, Gil thought. He situated the spear so that he was holding the tail end of it in his right hand. Then, after curling his arm around himself, he flung the spear like a Frisbee towards the flying saucer. It landed somewhere in front of Korben, causing a racket as it made contact with the ship's gleaming surface, and then began rolling down towards the edge. The alien, whose reaction must have been delayed with disbelief, lurched forward and grabbed it at the last possible moment. Gil cupped his hands over his mouth and took a deep breath.

"Go home, Korben," he shouted. "Just go home."

Korben held the spear in its right hand and stared at the tool for a moment as if it'd never seen it before. Then, hesitantly, it used the tool to pry the door back and quietly slip inside. The door shut with a loud bang, and after a few moments, the ship whirred to life and hovered into the air. As it rose up into the sky and disappeared out of sight, Gil was amazed to see that the bottom of the craft was invisible—on the ships underside, all he saw were blue skies.

"Good riddance," he muttered. Finally alone, Gil looked around and almost instantly recognized where he was. It was a nature reserve—in relatively close proximity to his home—which he remembered being notable for not having any particularly interesting nature to observe. He'd hiked a rough trail through it during the one week out of each year they open the gates, and was a little disappointed to find only common birds and small rodents. Now, though, he was grateful for every small creature he laid his eyes on.

Scanning the horizon around him, he spotted a highway overpass and walked towards it. After a short while, he cracked a smile, which grew into a giggle, and then a laugh. Before long, he was on his hands and knees, and then finally on his back, laughing hard with tears of joy streaming down his face.

CHAPTER SIXTEEN:
BLAME IT ON THE WEATHER

Gil gently laid the steak on the heated frying pan and smiled at the pleasant sound it made as it sizzled. He was initially surprised to have a taste for the red meat, considering it had been the only thing he'd eaten for over a week, and to an extent he never wanted to touch the stuff again—the thought of consuming raw beef made him gag. But prepared slightly differently—that is, fresh, heavily-seasoned, marinated, and *very* well-done—he found he actually had quite an intense craving.

He also found that he had a rather strong craving for fruits and vegetables, although he wondered if the yearning was born out of the paranoia of having scurvy. He thought a lot about it the week before, when he made the short two-mile walk home in his damp and dirty clothes. He looked and felt like a bum, and hoped to get home without being seen by anyone. But as he trudged onto his block, he was suddenly and loudly greeted by a man sitting in a chair on a porch a few doors down from his house.

"Gil?" the man shouted. "Gil Sanders, is that you?" Gil only stuttered for a moment, feeling a little awkward that the man seemed to know his name—he had no idea who the man on the porch was. But as the wheelchair-bound man rolled down the walkway, Gil eventually recognized it was his neighbor from the night he had been abducted. This was the late-night walker who had been sucked up into the air before falling back down to the ground. Now he sat in a wheelchair, both of his legs set with plaster casts. Despite this recognition, Gil still couldn't address him by name, because he'd never learned it. *How the hell does he know my name?* Gil wondered.

"Your legs are broken," Gil finally managed, nodding towards the man's lower half.

"What? Oh, right... never mind that," and he twirled his hand to move things along. "I mean, you got picked up and taken away by that thing! Where did it drop you? And where have you been? You..." he stifled a laugh, "you look like shit, you know."

Gil's eyes widened. "You saw it?"

"How could I have seen it? No, I saw the effects of it, though. Namely, you and, well..." then he whistled while pointing to his two legs.

Gil stared at the man's legs for a moment, stuttered some more, and then said, "I gotta go. We can talk about this in a little bit, maybe tomorrow, but I gotta go home. Uh... sorry. Bye." And Gil began walking away.

"Hey, wait!" the man called to him. "People have been looking for you!" But Gil only held up a hand as he walked away, acknowledging the man but making it clear he wasn't going to stop.

A few moments later, Gil wriggled through his bathroom window that never locked—the latch broke off a few months before and he hadn't gotten around to fixing it. His front door *was* locked, which told him right away that his neighbor was right and at least someone had indeed come looking for him during his kidnapping. When he got through the tiny opening and looked in the bathroom mirror, all he could do was laugh. His neighbor was right about that too: he did look like shit. His face was dirty, cut up, bruised, and covered in long, greasy facial hair. His clothes were permanently stretched out from the sweat and other fluids, making them appear a size too big on him. And his arm was covered in still-healing little holes that made him look like a drug addict.

His teeth were killing him, the spaces between them all packed tight with bits of raw meat. His gums were bright red and his breath was putrid. So the first thing he did was floss, and it was a painful experience that resulted in a lot of sensitive, bleeding gums. Then he brushed the hell out of his teeth. Twice. Afterwards, the toothbrush felt so full of gunk that he threw it away and took another from a box full of unopened toothbrushes under his sink—he'd nabbed them from a dentist's office that had just changed their firm name and thus had no use for the old customized brushes. He was smearing more tooth paste onto his new toothbrush for a third go at it when he heard the doorbell ring. He slowly shuffled through his house towards the front door, assuming it was his injured neighbor again, or perhaps his friend Daryl. But when he got to his front door and opened it up, he was speechless.

News vans from three different television stations and a growing collection of bystanders crowded behind two police officers. At the sidewalk, a man with a microphone said to a woman holding a large video camera, "We are outside the home of Gil Sanders, the man who witnesses say was carried away last week by the first-ever tornado reported here in Elk Grove. Nearly as shocking as his disappearance is the fact that the tornado was apparently invisible. This rarity occurs when a cyclone forms without enough dirt on the ground to make it observable. Now, neighbors have reported that the man returned to his home just moments ago, disheveled and disoriented, and—oh, there he is! Let's see what he has to say."

Gil looked out at them, tired as hell and embarrassed at his appearance, and timidly asked, "Can I help you?"

"Are you Gil Sanders?" one of the officers asked.

"Uh... yes?" Gil responded, with a raised eyebrow and an upward inflection that made it sound more like a question than a statement of fact.

A well-dressed woman with a microphone in her hand asked so

firmly, so loudly and with such annunciation that it was almost as if she were yelling at Gil, "How does it feel to survive being picked up by a tornado?" And without waiting for a response, she asked, "Where have you been for the last week?"

Gil's brow furrowed, and he responded, "Tornado?" He looked behind the reporter and saw not only his friends Daryl and Linda, but also his wheelchair-bound neighbor. The man had apparently made quite a few phone calls after Gil abruptly ended their conversation.

He thought hard. He once again recalled those famous abduction stories he'd pondered while aboard the spacecraft, and asked himself what kind of lives those alleged victims were leading nowadays. Some had gotten book deals... a few of those books were later turned into modestly successful movies... and even those lucky few were largely considered crazy people, or elaborate pranksters, or both. The rest of them were simply crackpots, and Gil had a feeling that would be the camp he'd be stuck in. The time for obtaining any proof—besides his souvenir drinking glasses—was long gone, and now all he had to go on was his memory of the experience. He wished he'd taken something with him, something more substantial, but it was too late.

He still had no regrets about letting Korben go, however; with the alien ship back in space and with Korben likely already digitized and on its way back home, the alien would show up shortly behind its travel companions and give an account. If they chose to stick to their decision to leave Earth alone forever, then all the better. But if they chose to come back and make official contact, hopefully Gil's decision to let Korben go after all they put him through would count for something. That's when Gil would share his story. Until then, he decided he'd much rather just get back to work and find someone to take the space next to Daryl's restaurant.

The reporter's questions came back to the front of Gil's mind, and the corners of Gil's mouth curled into a small smile. He was relieved that he didn't have to come up with a story that would explain away his absence. The idea that an invisible tornado had ripped through Elk Grove was ridiculous—though not nearly as ridiculous as being abducted by Martians—and they'd clearly made up their mind about what had happened. Any mention of aliens, and they'd surely take one look at his pockmarked arm before jumping to some conclusions. It would be an open-and-shut case. So he took a deep breath, and mostly lied through his teeth.

"I don't remember anything," he said calmly. "I don't remember a tornado, I don't remember being picked up, and I don't remember where I've been. One moment, I'm taking down my garbage cans, and the next, I'm waking up in a field in the nature reserve next to the highway. I walked home."

The crowd murmured to life as the three news reporters tried as hard as they could to gracefully squeeze past the two police officers at the opening to Gil's porch. The two groups began asking many of the same questions, though for different reasons. After patiently answering exactly as many questions as were necessary to get them to leave, the crowd dissipated, and soon only Daryl and his wife remained. He was happy to see them, but could no longer hide that he was exhausted and just wanted to eat something, clean himself off, and sleep for a day. Still, he reluctantly invited them in.

Daryl and Linda stood in Gil's kitchen as the filthy man dug around the refrigerator and pantry in search of food that was still edible. They asked an endless stream of questions which he answered without any comprehension, because he was so preoccupied. The couple had taken the liberty of tossing out the rotten fruit in his kitchen—bless their hearts—and only just yesterday came into the house to throw away the spoiled meats in his refrigerator. After drinking what felt like a gallon of water, he grabbed an unopened bag of pretzels and ate out of the bag. He assembled a peanut butter and jelly sandwich that he ate in no more than four bites. He fried up four eggs over medium and set them on a paper plate, which he then curved so that he could feed them into his mouth.

Linda finally shook him from his ravenous pursuit when she asked if they could take him somewhere, or go somewhere and bring him something to eat. He considered, then shook his head. With a gravelly voice thick with the phlegm of a freshly-eaten meal, he explained that he would go to the store and buy groceries tomorrow. He asked if they'd come over for dinner tomorrow night, to which they enthusiastically accepted. And then after a short pause, with Gil's tact completely gone, he told them he loved them and then politely asked them to please get the hell out of his house so he could take a shower and go to sleep. So they did. And he did.

Over an hour later, when Gil was finally cleaned, shaven, and bandaged, he walked towards his bed without so much as a single thread of fabric on his body. Crawling under his sheets, he started to wonder if he might favor sleeping on the ground, curled up in front of his fireplace since he'd been forced to do it for over a week, but couldn't even finish the thought before he fell asleep. He slept solidly and loudly for over fourteen hours.

He awoke the following afternoon with a high fever. After postponing his dinner with Daryl and Linda to the following day, he planned to stay in bed and sleep it off but awoke again a few hours later with a throbbing pain in his eyes. He recalled it as a symptom of the alien sickness from Korben's transmission, and reluctantly decided he had to visit a doctor. And after a brief examination, he was shocked and terrified to learn the hospital had contacted the Center for Disease Control.

When CDC staff members arrived, a nervous and sweaty Gil obediently answered questions about who he'd had contact with, and where he'd been, with mostly fake answers. The convenient tornado made an appearance in the conversation.

At last, after the CDC staff members had departed, his doctor revealed that Gil had been infected with Rift Valley Fever—a viral infection largely native to southern Africa and most commonly observed in cattle. As it turned out, the virus was usually transmitted to humans as a result of handling the raw beef from infected livestock.

Gil remained at the hospital for the following week while he received treatment to ensure the virus didn't spread. The nurses and doctors would later remember Gil as the most pleasant patient to visit the hospital in recent memory. They were surprised to have a case of such an obscure virus in the United States, but even more surprised that, when they told Gil what he'd contracted, he laughed out loud. *If only they knew*, Gil thought. One of Earth's most domesticated animals had been responsible for the near-extinction of an entire alien race.

When he was released a week later, he went straight to the grocery store.

Gil flipped the steak over and continued chopping lettuce for the salad he was putting together. He told himself it was going to be epic, and he probably had a dozen different nuts, berries, cheeses, and meats to dump onto the bed of greens. Later that night, eating with his friends and enjoying the best beer he'd ever tasted, they talked and laughed about what Gil had missed while he was gone and what it must have been like to wake up in a field with no idea how he got there. In the middle of what had to be his tenth assurance that he didn't remember anything, Daryl suddenly started laughing and interrupted him.

"I'm sorry, but what is that thing?"

"What's what?" Gil asked, though he had an idea he knew what Daryl was referring to.

"That!" Daryl exclaimed, pointing his finger. "That broken PVC pipe you're drinking out of."

Gil looked at his glass. The soft, pearlescent material formed a slender cylinder that rose up and tapered off to an edge like a juice box straw. He smiled and stated matter-of-factly, "It's a souvenir."

A NOTE FROM BEN

I decided to take a crack at writing a book as a sort of writing exercise, to see if I could make myself write more and do it faster. It took me about six months to write this short novel (to be honest, I wasn't even sure at first if it qualified as a novel. I looked up the minimum word count, and found that some sources claimed at least 50,000 words, while other sources said it was anything over 40,000 words. And because my novel is a bit north of 49,000 words, I went with the latter.), so I can't say for sure if I've become any faster at writing, but I can say for sure that I've discovered I really enjoy it.

The reason I went with aliens as a topic was because the stupid things terrified me. I mean, not all of them—I've loved the *Alien* series as long as I can remember, *Predator* was only ever thrilling, and *The Blob* was simply a horror movie. Even *Killer Clowns from Outer Space* failed to scare me as a kid. No, I mean the simple aliens—the "Greys" with the guitar-pick head and black, almond-shaped eyes. The aliens from *Communion*, *Close Encounters of the Third Kind*, and *Fire in the Sky* (Though those were closer to orange) were the worst offenders. Oh, and *E.T.* I always thought that little creep was scary, especially when it screamed. As an adult, I can totally get past the alien's appearance and appreciate it for the beautiful film that it is, but as a kid? No way.

Maybe my childhood fear had something to do with growing up in the 90s, when several primetime shows about alien abductions seemed to be so popular (maybe they were never popular, though—it's possible my dad just liked watching them and he was one of a dozen viewers total.) but they always gave me the creeps.

In particular, I remember shows like *Sightings*, which usually featured sad-looking people claiming to have been abducted. I remember a lot of dramatic stills of bloodied underwear, which had me rolling my eyes even as a young child, but something about it still freaked me out—it was a weird twist on monsters hiding in children's' closets, with the key difference being that instead of wanting to gobble kids up, they just wanted to stand over your bed and stare at you. I feared as a kid that I'd open a door and find one staring at me, whether the door led to a closet, a bathroom, or even the front door to a house.

My older brother caught wind of this after a while and got really good at scaring the crap out of me for several years. Before too long, though, he didn't have to try too hard; he would just whisper "Don't wake up," referencing a woman who set up a tape recorder before going to bed and found that phrase repeatedly uttered the next morning on the resulting tape, and I'd run off to tell mom. In hindsight, I guess it wasn't that hard to scare me.

My wife and I watched *Signs* for our first date when we were 17 years old. I wanted to watch it because I figured that it would be the kind of aliens I liked to see (Like in *District 9*, or *Prometheus*), and also because I figured it would scare her and she'd want to cuddle or something. What a fool—I slept with the lights on for a month. This is despite how silly they ended up looking and how improbable the twist was. And even now, at 31, I see movies like *Area 51*, *The Fourth Kind*, and *Extraterrestrial* popping up on Netflix, and I actively avoid them because I don't want to be a 31-year-old parent sleeping with the lights on in bed with my wife.

The point is that I've thought a lot about aliens, so while I technically ignored the age-old advice about writing what you know, I definitely wrote about what I thought about many times at night when I was a kid... and, you know, as an adult sometimes too.

Believe it or not, though, despite the fact that they creep me out, I have to admit I always felt unsatisfied with most of the abduction tales I've heard. They were usually too fuzzy—no one could remember exactly what happened, or sometimes their experiences would play out like an acid-fueled drug trip. So my goal in writing *The Waypoint* was to make Gil as lucid as possible throughout his experience, and I think I did a pretty good job of that. No telepathy (well, almost), no mystical wisdom, certainly no probing, and no vague conspiracies—these things have all entertained me at one point or another, of course, but they're simply not the sort of thing that kept me up at night as a child (right, and as an adult).

And speaking of being kept up at night, another personal benefit of writing this book is that aliens aren't as creepy as they used to be. Indeed, giving them names, mundane chores, and comparably average intelligence has demystified these otherwise very mystical childhood monsters. Of course, writing *The Waypoint* has also made it clear that virtually no one else finds these things scary. Would you believe I at one point thought I was writing a horror story? I always asked readers if the book scared them at all, and they always had to stifle a laugh. They assured me the book had moments that were gross, humorous, creepy, or thrilling, but that it was completely devoid of any horror. I suppose I can relate, though—vampires creep out my wife, which I've always found silly.

Writing this book was also a great learning experience on how to write. For one thing, I learned that this book has entirely too many adverbs. Like, however many adverbs one should limit themselves to in a book of this length, I have about four times that amount. Even in this short block of text, I have more adverbs than anyone should. Oops. If I manage to write another book, I think I'll be much more mindful of how many adverbs I'm using.

I also want to involve more characters in future stories. In the end, The Waypoint was a story about Gil and Korben. And I only had to make one of those characters talk. I want to have bigger conversations between more than two people, and I want some of them to be women—you may have noticed there was only one line in this book spoken by a female (a reporter), and it wasn't even an important line. So that's a goal.

My favorite parts of the book are when Gil was alone and interacting with stuff on the ship. It played out like a point-and-click adventure game, with him goofing around with things and seeing what would happen. Chapter Six was the best example of this. He had a couple hours to himself to go from room to room and be nosey. There was also a bit more of this later on, when he chucked a cube of meat at the spinning disc, and again when he found the birthing room.

Anyway, I sincerely hope you enjoyed this little tale I cooked up. Thank you for reading!